CW00642329

ISBN: 978-1-942857-50-1

❀ Created with Vellum

DESIRE

THE DANGEROUS BILLIONAIRE
JASPER BLACKSTONE

Z.L. ARKADIE

Author's Note

As of May 7, 2022, this book has been updated. The POV is now first-person present tense to improve readability and pacing. Also, story elements have been refined.

Also, as of August 15, 2022, the last name of the main family has been changed from Christmas to Blackstone.

Enjoy!

Hello, Goodbye

HOLLY HENDERSON

My legs grow weak, but I manage to remain standing. I can't remember if I already asked Jasper what's he doing here. Looking at him is so unreal. He's like a mirage appearing across the parched sands of a hot desert, an apparition haunting my office. I can't figure out my emotions right now. Or maybe I can. There are too many. Some good. Some horribly painful. I open my mouth to say something, anything, but he presses a finger over his lips, slips into my office and closes the door gently behind him.

He closes more distance between us and standing tall, asks, "How are you?"

I'm lost for words yet again. But look at him. He's still so very tall, dark, and handsome, even if he looks mentally drained. I want to say that I'm fine, but am I? How can I summarize the past few weeks in one simple word? I had been so angry at him ever since leaving the Blackstone manor. I spent days crying on my pillow. I hadn't had an appetite. I hadn't wanted to work. Then one morning, I suddenly had no more tears to give Jasper Blackstone. Rising from the ashes of my despair, I got out of bed, dressed, and dragged myself to the office. On that drive over, I persuaded myself to never think of Jasper again. *So why is he in my office, making my heart go pitter-patter?*

"What are you doing here?" I strain to say.

He takes a small step toward me, and I shoot both hands up, motioning him to keep his distance. I can't take his nearness right now. I'm not strong enough yet. Jasper stops in his tracks. His beautiful and tired eyes are glossed over with what appears to be confusion and a touch of sadness.

"You look beautiful," he whispers.

There's passion in his voice which sends vibrations through my soul. But I can't give in to the force that draws me to Jasper. Suddenly, I'm appropriately angry that he could say that to me after all this time. *How could he say that?*

"You never told me what you're doing here." My tone is sharp enough to cut him to pieces.

His eyebrows flash up like he's just realized something. "I hurt you. I'm sorry."

I shake my head defiantly. I cannot let Jasper Blackstone trap me again. His sister tried to warn me about him, but I didn't listen. I thought my heart was made of steel, but alas, it's flesh and blood, so easily smashed and ripped to shreds.

"I don't see how we have anything else to say to each other," I say, hoping to sound convincing. *I didn't, though. I know I didn't.*

"I came to see you. I've missed you." His voice is a desperate whisper.

I can feel his body reaching out to me as he reads my resolve. In the space between us, I visualize our souls embracing, kissing, remembering how it feels to be in each other's arms.

"Oh," I sigh.

The longer his gaze lingers on my face, the more uncomfortable I become. I fold my arms and drop my unfocused gaze. I don't hate him. I understand the complexities of his association with the Valentines. But he could've at least warned me—especially since his nemesis is Arthur Valentine. I've had a run-in with Valentine before, and it was scary,

3

very scary. But still… I don't hate Jasper—it would be impossible to hate him.

"Do you have any idea what happened to Bryn?" I ask, reaching for something to say. However, hope sits in the pit of my belly that he's the one who has her and is keeping her protected.

Jasper narrows an eye. "You've heard about Bryn?"

I nod. "Do you have any idea where she may be?" *Please say yes.*

He shakes his head. "But I'm looking into it."

"How?"

His head dips slightly which is his way of letting me know to pull back Miss Henderson, the reporter.

"I'm on it, Holly," he finally says.

I nod softly.

We gape at each other with nothing but every-thing to say to each other. He keeps watching me as though he's able to see past my flesh and bone and into my soul. And the thing is, we can stand here and gape at each other like this forever. The features of his face show his stress, and so does his strong and usually assured posture. His shoulders are hunched as though he's carrying the weight of the world upon them.

I want to touch him, make him feel better. "When was the last time you slept?"

Jasper shakes his head, holding his pinched expression. "I don't know. But I had to see you. I had to know if…"

One beat passes and then two. As usual, we leave what should be said, unsaid.

"So how's married life?" I ask.

A slight lift to the right side of his mouth is evidence that he knows I'm going fishing and he welcomes it. "I'm not married, Holly."

His answers strikes me in all the right places and my eyelids get stuck closed for a moment as relief spreads through me. "What about Arthur Valentine?"

Jasper's sexy lips tighten and then release. "What about him?"

"He was insistent that you follow through on whatever deal he made with your father."

The anger in his eyes burn bright. Then, as if he just remembered something, Jasper quickly glances across his shoulder. "I have to go."

"You're leaving?" I sound so sad, so lost.

His glossy eyes take me in. "I don't want anything to happen to you. I can't be seen here."

Reading between the lines, I press a hand over my heart. "Am I in danger?"

"You will never be in danger, Holly."

The way he's looking at me makes me believe him. Then, Arthur Valentine's daughter's face came to mind. "Are you still marrying Julia?"

"No," he replies without pause. Then, he quickly turns his back on me. "I have to go."

The door opens and I call his name in desperation. My heart pounds, not wanting him to leave my life just yet.

Thankfully, Jasper freezes. In the silence exists ache and yearning. I don't know what to say, though. I can't beg him to stay. I can't go with him either.

"I'll see you soon," he quietly says. "Also, keep to a steady routine. You're being followed."

"By who?" I gasp. But the answer suddenly falls into my head. Arthur Valentine is having me tailed.

Jasper turns the doorknob. "Goodbye, Holly."

"Wait," I call, my heart beating a mile a minute.

His back stiffens, giving me a moment to say, "Does Bryn's situation have anything to do with you not marrying Julia?"

He doesn't move or speak.

"What about Dale? Do you believe they're both

dead? Only blood was found and spread in a very controlled manner. Is that your take? Or do you have a different opinion?" Jeez, that comes out of my mouth so fast that I'm left breathless.

"As I said, we'll talk soon. Don't follow me."

And without another word, Jasper makes a quick exit.

I'VE BEEN SITTING AT MY DESK, STARING AT THE wall for quite some time. Seeing Jasper and then hearing about Bryn's disappearance suddenly renews my interest in the mysteries surrounding the Blackstone family. Suddenly, I know what to do. I call Rich at the lab in California to ask for the results of the DNA I collected and submitted two weeks ago.

Rich answers my call quickly. The first thing he says is that he's been waiting to hear from me. What he tells me next takes my breath away.

Chattanooga Here I Come

HOLLY HENDERSON

Gripped by tension, I squeeze the steering wheel tighter. What Rich told me was so insane that I couldn't sit on that information. I had to do something. Impulsivity took over me and now I'm on my way to Chattanooga, Tennessee.

After leaving my office, I didn't go home first to pack a bag. Since Jasper said I'm being watched, I made sure no one would see me make my escape.

I kept the lights on in my office as I packed my MacBook Pro and put on an oversized ankle-length winter coat and a beanie. I didn't wear either article of clothing to the office today. I keep all kinds of cold weather gear stored in a closet just in case it turns very cold at the end of the day, forcing me to layer-up to keep warm. So if whoever was watching me happened to catch a glimpse of a woman wearing a long coat and beanie, they probably would've assumed I was someone else. At least I hope so.

I took the stairs to the parking garage and slipped into the alley. Not a soul was around so I couldn't have been seen entering the medical offices which were three buildings down and on the opposite side of the alley. I hiked several blocks in the stifling cold, heading down the smaller city streets. I made sure to change it up by walking down one-way streets, being mindful of the differing directions of traffic flow. It would've been hard to tail me in a vehicle. I kept checking around me, making sure no one was tailing me on foot. A few blocks away from the rental car agency, I ducked into a CVS drugstore and bought a three-pack of bikini panties, a red out-of-season holiday sweater, and stretchy sweat pants, as well as a toothbrush, toothpaste, deodorant, and soap. I purchased a six-pack of bottled water then went into Subway and ordered a few turkey and cheese sandwiches, chips, and a chocolate chip cookie. Even though it was cold enough to freeze my eyebrows off, the brisk pace at which I walked and completed tasks generated enough body heat to keep me warm. Two blocks east later, I arrived at the rental car place. Jess behind the counter asked if I was renting for business or pleasure. I said, "Business." And she knew to charge my rental to the Rise account, which is an account shared by me and eleven other independent journalists. They put me in a four-wheel-drive vehicle fairly quickly and sent me on my way.

I've been stuck behind the wheel for the better part of six hours. Between portions of the highway being closed, traffic detours, and major and minor accidents, driving has been a nightmare. It's dark and I'm only in Harrisonburg, Virginia. I have a headache and I'm sleepy, and since it's best to reach my destination in the light of day, I pull into the parking lot of a decent and comfortable-looking hotel, where all the rooms are suites, and book one for the night.

———

MY ROOM IS ON THE TOP FLOOR OF A FOUR-STORY building. I'm looking out over a sparsely lit view of a flat, snow-covered field lined by tall pine trees. A shiver blushes through me even though I've already cranked up the heat. It's so cold outside. I've considered living in warmer climates on many occasions, but I can't see myself leaving the East Coast. I love the energy that exists on this side of the country. I want to be in the thick of it, and this is where the thick of it resides.

A lot is going on inside my head. I can't stop thinking about the Blackstones—Jasper in particular. I keep picturing how he looked the first time I walked into Amelia's room on accident. I don't know… I wonder if he knows what I learned.

Knock, knock, knock.

I jump startled, turning toward the door. Hand over my racing heart, I wonder who could that be. My glare lands on the clock sitting on the nightstand. It's 9:47 p.m. I wonder if I've been found by Valentine's goons. He has those—goons. One reason why my drive felt so arduous is I kept checking the rearview mirror to see if I was being followed. As far as I could tell, I wasn't.

I stand still, hoping the person had the wrong room, figured it out, and moved along.

The knocks come again, and there's something about the cadence that makes me frown with recognition.

I move quickly to the door and look through the

peephole. A face fills the frame. I gasp and take a large step back.

"Jasper, is that you?" I ask even though I already saw that it's him.

"It is." I can barely hear him.

I press my hand over my heart, contemplating what to do next. How in the hell did he find me here?

"Shit," I whisper.

I pause briefly before I open the door. My heart swells from seeing Jasper Blackstone in the flesh.

Reunited

HOLLY HENDERSON

My feet remain stuck to the carpet as the cold air from the hallway moves past me, eager to connect with my heated room.

"What are you …?" I ask.

Jasper checks nervously over his shoulder. "May I come in?"

I quickly step back to give him space to enter. His nearness overtakes me and I feel woozy for a moment. I can hardly believe he's actually here as I close the door.

"Where in the hell do you think you're going?" he asks before I could finish locking the door.

I turn and blink hard, wondering if he would

vanish into thin air at any moment. Him being here just doesn't feel real. "What?"

"You were supposed to lay low."

I wave off his concern. "Don't worry about me. I'm fine. But I'm just…" I shake my head. "Jasper, what are you doing here? And how did you find me?"

We stare at each other, both expecting answers from the other I presume. He's wearing the same black wool coat he had on in my office. I was so shocked to see him earlier that I hadn't registered how nicely dressed he is. His pants are black and expensive just like his shiny leather black boots with brown soles. Jasper is always put together so well. He cares how he looks. I inhale his mouthwatering scent—umm, delicious.

"Where are you on your way to?" he finally asks.

I clamp my lips. My first inclination is to not directly answer his question since he hasn't yet explained why he followed me. However, I close my eyes and inhale deeply to start thinking with my brain and not my broken heart. The prudent thing to do is treat Jasper like a source and not the man who hurt me.

I stand tall and confident. "Chattanooga, Tennessee."

He narrows one eye. "What for?"

His expression is so sexy that all I want to do is kiss him. So I take another breath. This time the goal is to quell my lust. That doesn't do the job so I steer my gaze away from his face and onto the trampled carpet. "I'm still investigating your family," I admit.

The silence in his lack of response is deafening. I look up, he's scrutinizing me. I sense he wants me to say more about investigating his family, and at this point, I don't mind sharing what I know. Heck, he's followed me out of the city and to this small hotel off the highway. We're already in this together.

I sigh. "I'll tell you everything."

Jasper's Adam's apple bobs as he nods. He takes off his coat and lays it across his bulging crotch as he sits on the foot of the bed. "I'm listening."

My breaths are uneven as lust soars through me. He's ready, and frankly, so am I. But hopefully I can get through this encounter with him without screwing him.

Hopefully.

His sweater is nice too.

Is it cashmere?

Oatmeal colored, cashmere.

I nod delicately and sit in the chair near the door. Keeping a clear distance from him helps my thoughts flow better, especially since we can't take our eyes off each other. And since our eyes are the windows to our souls, it's easy to see that we're having the same thoughts.

I clear my throat and look down at my lap, purposely breaking eye contact. "Well, a source told me your father often visited the home of a family who lived in Chattanooga, Tennessee." I look up to see how well he digested that bit of information.

He has that same look on his face that I've come to learn. He's not reacting. He wants to hear more. Goodness, he has the sexiest poker face I've ever seen. I would expect him to ask about the family, but Jasper Blackstone is too smart to do that. He wants me to keep talking, put all my cards on the table before he shows me his.

"Do you know of any family in Chattanooga that your father might have dealings with?" I ask.

"No," he says with a reserved calmness.

I tilt my head slightly. "No?"

"I said no, Holly."

Should I tell him about the DNA results?

Now we both have on our best poker faces. I suspect his was sexier than mine. I took a few more moments to contemplate whether I should give him the earth-shattering news about the DNA results. At some point he has to know. It might as well be now. I narrow an eye suspiciously—unless he already knows.

"What?" he asks, reading my expression.

I twist my mouth thoughtfully and then shift to sit on the edge of my seat. "So I got the results back from those DNA samples I told you about a few weeks ago."

He leans away from me. "And what did you find?"

"None of you have the same mother."

"Oh, I see," he says indifferently.

His coolness is proof that my suspicion was true. "You knew?" I sound disappointed because I am, especially if he kept the truth away from Bryn.

After a moment of staring at me, Jasper wipes his face with both hands. Then he stops rubbing to look at me. "Yes, I did."

I can't stop shaking my head. I'm so angry. "So when I told you a few weeks ago that I'd collected your family's DNA, you knew what I would discover?"

He nods. "Yes."

I heave a sigh. "Then why have me go through the motions?"

"Shit, Holly, I never committed to helping your unauthorized investigation of my family."

That's true. But still…

"Okay, then." I speak through my teeth with restraint. "Do your siblings know they have different mothers?"

"No," he says. "Well… Yes. One of them knows."

"Which one?" I ask real quick to get him to blurt the answer before realizing he spoke it.

But Jasper Blackstone will never fall for that kind of trick. Instead, his poker face is back, and it's sexier than ever.

We stare at each other. I see his eyes turning. Soon, we're going to be on top of that bed together. I just know it. But now, I need more answers.

"Why do they have different mothers?" I ask.

His eyes narrow to slits. He's showing me an expression that says the answer is for him to know and me to find out.

I sigh, frustrated. "Okay. Do you know what I'll find in Chattanooga, Tennessee? I mean, at least save me from this miserable drive."

He laughs softly. "As I said, I don't know anything about the family you mentioned. But keep me in the loop, and let me know what you find." His tone is demanding, and his attitude downright entitled.

"Why should I keep you in the loop?" I snap.

"Because I need to know what you discover to keep you safe."

I felt my eyebrows pull. "That makes no sense whatsoever."

Jasper remains the pillar of calm as he pats the empty space beside him. "Sit here."

"No," I say in a lust tainted whisper.

He pats the mattress again. "Come on. Just sit next to me, babe."

I want to sit next to him—Lord knows I do. But my head feels like it's exploding from indecision. Nothing has been resolved between us. Sleeping with him can hurt more than it already has. I don't think I can endure more heartache. His bedroom eyes drip with lust. It's no mystery why he wants me to sit beside him.

I close my eyes and shake my head continuously. "I can't."

"Why not?" There's a plea in his tone.

"You hurt me," I whisper.

The bed creaks, then he's standing in front of me. I look up. Jasper hands are out. He wants me to take them and God help me, I do. That was too easy for him.

He helps me to my feet. I cannot resist him as he wraps his arms around my waist. My lips were touching his. The taste of his tongue, which I've yearned for since our last kiss, saturates my mouth. It's as if I'm floating on air and soaring higher than the moon and stars.

"I missed you," he whispers before his tongue dives deep into my willing mouth.

He's lifting me off the floor and I'm pinched against his hard chest, torso and cock.

I can't say that I miss him back though—even though I miss him like crazy. Instead, I resist crying tears of elation. But then we shift into automatic pilot mode. Jasper lifts my sweater over my head, and I let him. His eyes devour my breasts, which are restrained by my bra. Carefully, he lifts the material from over my left nipple and sucks the tip, sending a tingling sensation through my breast that journeys to my lady parts.

Jasper, no! I think but can't say.

"Jasper, yes," escapes me in a whisper.

That's all it takes. Our hands and mouths are

famished for each other. If I thought my body and soul had lost all their passion for Jasper Blackstone, I was wrong. He guides me across the carpet, lays me down on top of the bed, and then spreads himself on top of me. Our bodies tangle as we go at it hot and heavy.

But what I'm feeling is more than the raw lust. Every stroke of his hand and swirl of his tongue around mine stirs my soul. We groan and whimper in each other's mouths. Then, he takes my jeans off after I kicked off my ankle boots. Jasper drops his trousers and steps out of them. His manhood presses against his underwear, eager to be set free. I cream at the sight of his cock, knowing it will soon be inside me. I smirk at him, showing pure desire. Jasper's electric eyes caress me with hunger and adoration.

I reach between my breasts to unclip my bra.

"Let me do it," he says with a sense of urgency.

He frees my breasts, and then takes my bra by the straps and slides it down my shoulders and arms. For a moment he seems unfocused. He wants to suck my nipples but finish undressing too. The choice is made when he takes off his shirt. Oh, how I'd missed the hills and creases of his muscular chest. And his six-pack... I slide my fingers down his gradient and he sucks air from the power of my touch. Jasper Blackstone is the ultimate man, strong and firm.

All that can be heard is our voracious breathing, sighing, and gasping. He drops to his knees, curls his arms around my thighs, and tugs my sex against his mouth. That was unexpected. But a pleasurable delight as I sigh, falling back onto the bed.

Jasper's soft brushing motion with his tongue makes an immediate impact. I cry out and dig my fingers deep into the over-laundered bed sheets. My cries of delight echo through the room. I suspect the walls are thin. Even though pleasurable sensations spark inside me, I take care to lower my voice.

"Mm…" I grunt, biting down on my back teeth as he brings me closer to climaxing.

I force myself to look at him. See what he's doing and how he's doing it. Our eyes connect as I gasp on air. *Look at him though…* Jasper loves watching what he was doing to me, relishing in his handiwork. He's so sexy.

"Oh…" I toss my head back as pleasurable vibrations expand through my sex. The feeling so hot, so delicious that I smash a pillow over my face and scream against it.

I toss the pillow and breathe heavily as Jasper

parts my knees. Feeling like a sex goddess, I slide my finger up and down my drenched slit. I have no idea what has gotten into me but I want to seduce him, make him needier for me. And it works because he licks his lips at the sight of my glistening slit. I lie back as he ceremoniously positions his body between my legs, and slides his cock, slow, indulgently and deep inside me.

My moan shivers. It feels so divine to be full of Jasper Blackstone yet again. He pumps in and out of my warmth and wetness. We gaze into each other's eyes. I cannot look away from him. He cannot look away from me.

"You're so—" He sucks air hard through his clenched teeth. And when he exhales, he tosses his head back and calls, "Oh!" as his body quivers.

THE ROOM IS COMFORTABLY WARM. JASPER AND I are naked as two jaybirds. All that can be heard is our breathing mingled with snow pelting the window. We hadn't said a word to each other since he gathered me in his arms after he exploded inside me. Being close to him feels good, but I can't stop frowning. There's something desperate about the way he's holding me. It's like he were trying to avoid a finality that we both see coming. I'm on a mission, and apparently so is he.

"What are you thinking?" he asks.

My eyes grow wide. What am I thinking? I want to stay like this forever. That's what I'm thinking.

"I was wondering if you're even slightly curious about what I'll find in Chattanooga," I say instead.

He pulled me even closer. Another inch, and I will disappear into his body.

I feel him shrug against me. "Not really."

"Why not?"

"My father had relationships with many people all over the country. If there was something in his dealings that should've concern me, I would know by now." He sounds so sure of himself which is so Jasper-like.

I roll my eyes even though I want to kiss his cocky mouth. "People have secrets, you know?"

"Yes, I do know."

"Maybe your father was keeping a secret. The Greers are very poor, and your father was very rich."

He chuckles before flipping me on my back, spreading my legs, and stuffing a fresh erection inside me.

I sigh at the first thrust, feeling every inch of his super-sized cock filling me. What a way to end an unwanted conversation. His cock continues thrusting with precision, letting me know he's focused on me. Jasper wants me to come, hard, fast, and long. His wish is my command as I guide my hips toward his strokes. The first blooms of an orgasm fill my womanhood. I close my eyes and concentrate on making the sensations flourish.

"Is that good, baby?" he whispers huskily.

"Mm-hmm." My eyes squeeze tightly shut, and the back of my head presses against a pillow.

"Speak. Let me hear you tell me, baby." He humps me better, faster.

Sensations build and build. I gasp and suck air until…

"Ah!" I cry.

"Say you love it," he demands, riding me with more intensity.

"I love you, baby," I freely claim.

Then my eyes open wide. *Did I say I love him? I did.*

From the dazed look on Jasper's face, either he hadn't heard me, or he doesn't care. *What the hell am I doing?*

I push against his chest. "Jasper, stop."

He doesn't hesitate to do as I ask. "What is it?" He's breathing heavily, clearly alarmed by my sudden change of mood.

"What are we doing?" I sound way too vulnerable for my liking. I'm risking a lot, by lying under Jasper Blackstone as he makes beautiful love to me. All the variations of our sex are making me fall deeper and deeper in love with him. And I can't feel this way about a man whose availability is questionable.

"What's wrong, baby," he says, looking so very confused.

"Didn't you hear what I said?"

He looks at me with his mouth open, as if at any moment he will come, and come hard.

I turn away from his beautiful yet confused eyes. "I don't want to do this anymore."

Jasper eases his engorged cock out of me and flops down on his back beside me. "What's going on with you?"

I press my forearm over my eyes. "I shouldn't have let this happen between us, but I couldn't stop it."

"Why shouldn't you let me make love to you?"

It's time to be brave. The moment has come to just say it.

"Because this thing between us is too deep. One day you'll marry someone else, and I'll love another."

Suddenly, Jasper reached out and pulled me against him. "You belong to me, Holly Henderson. Got it?"

I didn't get it.

"Got it?" he demands.

I sit up quickly, breaking free from his embrace. "I belong to you? Are you aware of how insane you sound?"

"I'm very sound, Holly," he says as though he's offended by my question.

"You don't get to be married to another woman while I belong to you," I say, purposely laying it on thicker. I want him to do something wild and crazy like grab hold of me, squeeze me tightly, and declare his eternal love for me rather than Arthur Valentine's daughter.

"You're a journalist," he says.

My frown intensifies. "You can't be with me because I'm a journalist?"

"Please stop twisting my words to suit your suppositions. Your profession makes you believe speaking truth to power is the most effective way to right wrongs."

I lean away from him. "Talk about suppositions."

"All I'm saying is that you do what you do as a journalist, and let me do what I do."

"And what is it that you do?"

The long silence is suddenly interrupted by two rings, the room phone and another that comes from Jasper's jacket. He jumps out of bed to answer his call while I answer mine. *Talk about being saved by the bell.*

More Mr. Blackstone Please

~~~
HOLLY HENDERSON
~~~

"Okay, thank you," I say to the front-desk clerk, who just informed me that the roads are closed, and because of it, the hotel will allow me to stay an extra night at no charge.

Jasper, who put on his coat and pants, took his call in the hallway. My mind raced with reasons why he would want privacy. The call definitely isn't from another woman or Julia Valentine. Jasper isn't a cheater. Plus, how many times does he have to tell me that he'll never marry her. But what will he do in return?

Here's what I know about Jasper Blackstone…

Here's what I always knew…

Jasper Blackstone is dangerous. His enemies fall and he's hard to catch.

He's still outside on his call but I can't hear him. Now that I'm alone, I grab my iPhone and perform a quick Internet search on Jasper Walker Blackstone, but this time I added the word "wife." The results that come up have to do with him being one of the sexiest and richest bachelors in the world. There's also an article that mentions why being single could hurt his chances at winning the presidency. Then there are rumors of him possibly being gay. I roll my eyes. That's totally untrue.

I narrow my eyes at the door. Where is he, and who is he talking to? The fact that he's been gone for so long gives me time to try another search.

Jasper Blackstone girlfriend.

All the results are about his brother Spencer. He's a playboy. However, there's something else that captures my attention.

Finally, the door opens, and I jump, smashing my phone against the bed sheets. Jasper's tall and manly frame walks into the room. He looks as pale as a ghost.

"What is it?" I ask.

He shakes his head while taking off his coat. "It's nothing."

I can see it's clearly something.

"What did the front desk want?" he asks.

"We're snowed in for the rest of the evening. She'll let me know when the roads are clear, but it looks as though we won't be able to travel tomorrow either." I haven't considered until now how awkward it will be remaining trapped in a room with Jasper for God knows how long. At some point, I could accidentally end up telling him I love him again. I wonder if he heard me the first time. Of course he had.

Jasper grunts thoughtfully as he lays his coat across the chair. "It does look pretty bad out there."

He takes his shirt off, and I'm momentarily stunned by the sight of his smooth skin, rippled chest, waist, abs, and arms. The chorus of his bravura nearly takes my breath away. I watch him as if he is a bronze statue who requires admiration as he walks into the bathroom.

"So who called you?" I ask.

"It was business," he says from the other room.

I smirk naughtily. "Private business."

He winks at me. "It's the only kind as far as you're concerned."

His pants are off as he falls onto the bed and rolls me on top of him. I'm suspended against his hard body and his erection grinds against my hood.

"So how about we pick up where we left off," he whispers sensually.

I swallow hard and nod. Our mouths melt, and I let go of all of my hang-ups.

MANY HOURS LATER

I call out to the Almighty as my sixth, maybe eighth, orgasm ripples through me. Goodness, Jasper knows how to make a woman come hard and fast. We've fucked in at least one-hundred-and-one ways too. My body aches. My sex throbs. I will be feeling Jasper Blackstone inside me long after we part ways.

He crawls up the bed and lies beside me, gathering me in his arms.

"Um." I writhe, still feeling the aftereffects of climaxing.

Jasper kisses, nibbles, and licks me on his favorite spot on my back.

"Holly, I love being with you," he says.

There goes that word again—love.

I yawn. "I know." Of course he loves sexing me.

There was no way I can deny it. The feeling is mutual.

Then I remember what I saw during my second Internet search of him. "Hey," I say quite spiritedly. "I read somewhere that Randolph Black-stone died two days ago. We both know that's not true. Why did you wait so long to announce his death?"

He tenses against me. "You knew we had to keep it quiet for a while."

"Right, but two weeks? That's a long time."

Again, he's quiet, and I'm beginning to learn that silence for Jasper is caution. "I had to tie up some loose ends."

"What sort of loose ends?"

"Listen, babe, we trusted you enough to let you in on our private family matters. Don't make me regret it."

I scoff. "I hope you're not here managing me with sex."

"What? No," he says as though he's insulted. "I don't want the truth to surface in some newspaper."

"I wouldn't do that, and you know it."

"No, I do not."

I want to push him away from me while at the same time disappear into his body. "Well, Bryn knows. I kept all of her secrets in college. I'm good at that—keeping secrets."

He holds me tighter, and I let him, even though the body heat our closeness generates makes me want to beg for a hit of coolness.

"So, did those loose ends you had to tie up have anything to do with you marrying Julia Valentine?" I ask.

He remains silent for a few beats. "Are you asking that as my lover or a reporter?"

I frown. "Is that all I am to you, your lover?"

He sighs forcefully. "Holly, come on."

"Come on, what?"

"You mean a lot to me. How many times do I have to say it before you believe it?"

"Talk is cheap."

"Then what do you want from me?"

Ask me to marry you. Of course, that was silly. I've only known Jasper for three weeks.

"You could initiate a plan for our future together or something. Basically, I want you to make an effort that lets me know you want to be with me full-time."

"I'm here, aren't I? This is a huge effort." He grinds against me with his blossoming erection.

"Jasper, really? You're doing that when we're discussing this?"

He chuckles. "Baby, just let me slide in when I'm ready. I have to be inside you."

"You're doing me as if it's your last time," I blurt. Finally, I say what's been bothering me ever since he'd returned to the room after his phone call.

Jasper pushes his new erection between my thighs, and I gasp as he enters my wetness from behind. "Whenever I make love to you, it feels like the last time," he whispers as his cock slides in and out of me.

"Just wait." I jut my hips forward and away from his insatiable manhood.

His hips chases mine. "Wait for what, baby?"

I remained very still.

Jasper kisses my earlobe. "Don't go anywhere, please. How many times have I told you that I'm falling in love with you?"

I sigh sharply. "Tell me what you like about me other than my body and fucking me."

He prods me a few times with his cock and I sigh. That feels so good.

"When you talk clever, that gets me excited. That's one of a number of things I like about you."

"What else do you like about me?" I whisper. *Umm…*

"You're loyal, curious, and sweet, so damn sweet," he moans.

I take that he means "sweet" as a double entendre.

There's no more talking, only sighing, moaning, and whimpering until Jasper shakes with orgasm. Then, we are forced to let go of each other so our bodies can cool. We don't fall asleep, though. Jasper and I lay on our sides, facing each other. He asks me about growing up in Northern California. I tell him all about my father and mother and how they would move into a new community, scam all the neighbors out of as much money as they could, then disappear.

"That's why I never made friends. I felt like a parasite. I wanted to knock on doors and warn everyone in the world to not trust my parents, especially my father. But I couldn't do that. I felt so helpless. All I could do was watch."

"Parents are people, babe, and people have their shit to deal with. Having children doesn't change that. But you're a smart woman. I'm sure you know that already."

I crack a tiny smile. I loved how he makes me

feel so astute, as if I can recite the *Webster's Dictionary* by heart. I want to convince him that I'm more of a survivor than an intellectual, and the difference is marked, but I don't want to kill that glimmer of appreciation in his eyes.

I continue to tell him about my life. "When we moved to Pittsburgh, I ended up in an amazing high school. The school counselor is now a world-renowned cognitive behavioral therapist. I used to have sessions with her twice a week. That's when I learned what you just said."

"I wish I could've seen you back then."

We smile lovingly at each other. Goodness, he's a beautiful man. It takes every ounce of control in my body to not jump his bones yet again. But I'm sore. We've already fucked too much.

"What about you? I bet growing up a Blackstone was quite interesting."

"It was miserable," he says without pause, which I found surprising. His eyes aren't guarded either.

I'm not going to ask him to elaborate, even though I want him to. I picture a pretty little boy standing next to his perpetually scowling father, both wearing three-piece suits.

"I was taught to live by Randolph's rules and

never my own ever since I could remember," he says.

"Isn't that what rich men like your father are all about? Control?"

He swallows what must be a lump in his throat. "Yes," he barely says.

There are memories playing behind his eyes, I can see them. I wonder what he endured under the harsh palm of Randolph Blackstone. During my stay in the Blackstone mansion, I noticed whenever the subject of their father's declining health arose, Bryn, Asher, and Spencer had the luxury of being more distant about the impact of what that meant for the future of their family. Jasper, on the other hand, seemed to carry the weight of the changes that were before them. At first, it had just been an inclination of mine, but then on Christmas Eve, on the day of their father's death, I noticed something about them all. They all glowed. They couldn't escape the confines of that mansion fast enough. And then they were gone. Jasper was the last man standing, and I had left him alone. I should have stayed. I should have fought for us.

Jasper smiles lightly—I assume to assure me he was okay. "Once, when I was about nine or ten, I had a teacher. I can't remember his name, but he gave us a lesson on space and NASA needing brave boys and girls like us to choose a career in discovering uncharted territory. I liked the idea of going where no man's ever gone. I came home from school and told my father I wanted to be an astronaut and told him all about my lesson." His eyes grow dim. "Randolph grabbed me by the neck and pinned me to the wall. I was homeschooled after that."

I reach out and run my fingers across his succulent bottom lip. He quickly captures my hand and kisses the back of it before drawing me against him. The way he holds me and how I feel in his embrace signals a change in our relationship. The moment satiates me just the same as if we were making beautiful love. Perhaps that is exactly what I'm feeling at the moment. Jasper's engulfing presence is beginning to erase the parts of me that never let a man close enough to love me. I have never felt safer than I do now, and soon I fell asleep.

At some point, I see Jasper at the Christmas party at the Blackstones. He's walking the floor, his arm linked with Julia Valentine's. They greet their guests. Even Asher takes Julia's hand and kisses the back of it like an adoring fan. I watch from a distance as they make their approach. I wonder if

Jasper will acknowledge me. They shake more hands and laugh with more of their guests. I wait my turn.

Bryn sidles up next to me. "I told you not to have sex with him. Well, that's why."

When I turn to look at her, half of her head is missing, and she's bleeding profusely.

I gasp. My eyes pop open, and I wake up to a lit room. "It's only a dream," I whisper in an effort to comfort myself. It takes a moment to remember that I shouldn't be alone. However, the space beside me is empty.

I sit up swiftly. "Jasper?" I call, casting my voice toward the bathroom. My gaze falls on the pillow Jasper had slept on. There's a small square sheet of paper ripped from the hotel notepad.

Oddly, the first thing I notice is Jasper's handwriting. It's the first time I've seen his elegant penmanship. Then I read the words.

DEAR HOLLY,

I apologize for leaving so soon.

Know that I care deeply for you.

And you are mine. And I am yours.

Always,

Ace

"Ace," I whisper as a knot forms in my chest and my sinuses swell.

Why didn't he sign his rude goodbye note as Jasper?

I can't help being equally intrigued and angry. But I refuse to let myself cry. I'm lucky. My heart doesn't ache, at least not yet. I'm just numb. And that's a feeling I want to bottle up and keep with me until I'm ready to tell Jasper Blackstone to go to hell.

The Clean Up Man

❧

JASPER BLACKSTONE

I stare out the window of Blackstone Family Enterprises, or BFE, headquarters in Lower Manhattan. My view is a sliver of the Hudson River and another tall glass skyscraper of equal size. It's not remarkable, and that's the point. The old man considered taking a moment to admire a view a waste of an emotion. Instead, he wanted his executives imprisoned by the drive to line their pockets with the cash he so freely offered, but only if they did whatever he ordered without question. A building blocking a skyline seemed a small sacrifice for bending to Randolph's desires.

I smirk as I recall that before Randolph became ill, I was about to initiate a hostile takeover. But now, I don't have to do that. The entire Blackstone family fortune was smartly left to one living descendent in efforts to preserve the family's wealth. Now it was all his. BFE is mine and everything we own is mine. Not my brothers' or my sister's—mine.

But I will take care of my siblings until we all die, and they know it. Because that's exactly what I've been doing for all of our lives.

I think about Holly, and her climaxing beneath me, her walls shivering around my cock. Why the fuck didn't I wake her up and do her one last time before going. I couldn't find the words to explain to her that now is not the time to flaunt our relationship in the open. Of course she knows that. Holly is a smart woman, a realist. That's why I fucked up. I should've waken her up. I should've made love to her one more time.

Arthur Valentine has to be dealt with and swiftly. When Valentine had shown up at the mansion on Christmas Day, with his daughter in tow, I had known one thing for sure. Arthur was a desperate man. I let Holly escape for her own safety, but every molecule that comprises my being wanted to chase after her and convince her to stay. A man ultimately knows when he's found the one. She's the one for me.

On the afternoon Holly had stopped her car at

the front of the mansion, I hurried outside to tell her to go home. William had just informed me that we would be hosing another guest for five days. When he'd said her name, I knew exactly who she was. We were in no way prepared to accommodate an award-winning investigative journalist. Randolph was on his deathbed, and it was incumbent on the entire household to keep that quiet. Important business deals were in the works. By then, Randolph was merely a figurehead who the world thought still called the shots. I needed everyone to keep believing just that. I feared a reporter of Holly's caliber would be able to see through our façade in less than twenty-four hours. I knew she was Bryn's friend. But it didn't take long to figure out that she would be loyal to Bryn, and ultimately to my family. That's why I couldn't help but fuck the daylights out of her. I want her right now on my desk. Then I would take her to lunch. I'd show her off. She's beautiful. So damn beautiful. So damn soft. So damn smart, inviting, and kind. *I love her.* And today is the day I make sure I keep her forever.

Heads will soon roll.

Was my father the devil? The answer to that question is the reason I chose not to halt Holly's investigation into my family. I trust her to answer the questions I'd been too afraid to prove.

Randolph Blackstone had a darkness. Whenever I looked into my father's eyes, I could see his void, his abyss staring back at me. Thank God I've managed to keep our father's darkness from rubbing off on my siblings. They are wounded, but they're not damned.

Miraculously, I have been able to keep the Blackstone family image intact despite Randolph's insistence on destroying it. But I hadn't stepped foot in the Lower Manhattan office in three years, two months, and eight days. This office had been my father's playland. The men who worked here were the worst of the worst and not the best and the brightest. They were misogynistic, greedy, and soul-less assholes who would do whatever it took to win. But they will all be gone soon. And they will not be able to hurt my family because I have been stalking them, finishing them, and they hadn't even known it.

"Mr. Blackstone," Jacqueline, the office secretary, calls.

He slowly turn to see the curvy, wide-eyed beauty, who is the star of most men's sexual fantasies. Not mine, though. Holly Henderson is my one and only star. Jacqueline stands in the doorway. She's the general prototype of women who works in our offices at this building. And that's not by accident.

"Yes?" She bristles from my sharp tone. "How may I help you?" That's better, more genial.

She maintains a steadfast composure. "Sir, Brett keeps asking for an agenda. I could whip up one quickly, an impromptu one."

I study the stressful look on her face. I've been working in the office for the past week. The guys here are into ordering the assistants around, all of whom are female, as if they're indentured servants. It sickens the hell out of me. I imagine Bryn being one of those women, and it makes me want to kill somebody.

"Didn't I say there will be no agenda?" *Shit.* My tone can freeze fire. I'm working on lightening up, especially for Holly.

Again, Jacqueline pulls her shoulders back to stand taller. "Yes, sir."

There's something about her that's off. I can tell that it's not natural for her to take a subservient role.

I watch her with laser focus. "How long have you been working for this company?" I ask.

Her eyebrows ruffle, and then lift. "Six years, Mr. Blackstone."

"In my book, that gives you seniority over a weasel like Brett, who's barely hanging onto his job."

Jacqueline's lips part as though she has no idea how to respond to that.

"I'm telling you there's no agenda. What you tell him is on you. Because you are his superior. Just know that you can tell him to go eat shit and keep your job." I wink at her.

Jacqueline's eyes look dazed and then she clears her throat. "Yes, and um…"

"No agenda," I bark, figuring she's having a problem saying no to the assholes who worked at this location, which is one reason why all of them had to go.

She nods swiftly. "I understand, sir. But, um, also, some of the assistants wanted to know if Christmas bonuses were going to be distributed this year."

I frown. "You haven't gotten them yet?"

"No, Sir."

"Don't call me that. Refer to me as Jasper or Mr. Blackstone, but not sir."

I always hated the rule that all the assistants,

who are female, are required to call their bosses, all male, "sir." I tried to convince Randolph of the legal ramifications of such a decree, but he had been dogmatic about keeping it. Whenever I tried to convince my father to change the way they operated in these parts, Randolph's darkness glared at me, warning me to not mess with his plaything or else. So I left the Lower Manhattan office completely in his hands. For me, it was out of sight, out of mind. But now I'm fully in charge, and that means the madhouse is about to turn into what I have termed the "sane asylum."

"Yes, I will call you Jasper," Jacqueline says timidly.

"Good. And let the assistants know they'll have their bonuses with interest. I would also like to meet with all of you after I wrap up with the executives and board." I twist my wrist to check the time on my watch. "Set the assistants' meeting for two p.m."

"Yes, Jasper. Is that all?"

I like how she said my name like she was trying out her new freedom. I crack a smile. "Yes, that will be all."

Jacqueline briskly nods. "Oh, I almost forgot. What about this?"

She hands me a manila folder. I open it, skim its contents and sigh.

"Should I send it out?" she asks.

It's part of the temporary deal I made with Arthur to manage him.

"Yes," I say even though I'm worried how Holly's going to react to the news.

Jacqueline says, "thank you," then rushes back to her desk.

I turn in the direction of the conference room. It's finally time. All hell is about to break loose.

A Trip To Chattanooga

HOLLY HENDERSON

Nine hours after the front-desk clerk assured me the roads are clear, I arrive at another hotel in downtown Knoxville, Tennessee. The valet parked my car, and now I'm stepping in to the elevator after booking a suite with a jetted tub for the night. I need a long, hot bath. I could've forced myself to drive all the way to Chattanooga, but my eyes and brain have taken me as far as I can go on a snowy day of road closures and slowdowns due to traffic accidents. Plus, I don't want to arrive in the city too exhausted to be an effective investigator. I also have my regular work to dive into. But during my drive, for me, it's not smart to talk on the phone and drive in the snow, even if I use the hands-free mechanism. I let a number of calls go to voice mail, never checking to see who was trying to contact me. Deep down, I hoped one of the callers was Jasper, apologizing and expressing his devoted love.

I stare at the lit numbers on the elevator panel and count up to the eleventh floor. I haven't cried over him yet. Maybe because he really hasn't given me anything to weep over.

The elevator doors slide open, and I fight the urge to picture Jasper standing in the hallway, waiting to kiss me. But no one is in the hallway, not a peep can be heard as I drag my tired and achy body up the carpeted corridor. I stretch my neck and my torso, thinking, wow, our marathon sex has left me feeling as if I've been training for a triathlon or something.

As soon as I enter my room, I fire up my MacBook Pro and sit it on top of the bed. I strip out of my clothes, including my underwear, wrap myself in the complimentary fluffy white robe, and slide my feet into the slippers. I brush my teeth, wash my face, and fight the urge to take a warm bath before working. I know if I soak in the water, my exhaustion would turn into sleepiness, and I wouldn't be able to stay awake.

After wrapping my hair in a messy bun on top

of my head, I cuddle up against the headboard with my computer and log into my hot spot. My search alerts ding as soon as I'm connected to the Internet, notifying me of recent news.

One story is about Jasper Blackstone and Blackstone Family Enterprises. It's a story about mass firings following Randolph's death.

For a moment, I question why I'm even continuing the exploration into the Blackstones' past. Jasper never explained why they all had different mothers. I could understand why Amelia and Randolph had kept the truth of Bryn, Asher, and Spencer's parentage a secret, but then I couldn't. They are a family who travels through veiled hallways in their creepy mansion. I still don't quite understand the relationship between Spencer, Asher, and Gina. It seems sick but then it also seems as if they're all wounded birds with clipped wings. I don't know. However, one thing is true, the Blackstones are a powerful and duplicitous family with enough secrets to fill a stadium.

"So why not tell Asher, Spencer, and Bryn the truth?" I whisper. Wait—but one of them knows the truth. It's not Bryn, and I'm sure that if Asher knows, he would've told Bryn a long time ago. From understanding the twins are very close. So it has to be Spencer. He knows?

Damn. It's just as I had figured, the Blackstones have secrets beneath secrets and then a million more beneath those. That's why I continue to pursue the investigation or the story. My natural inclination to be inquisitive won't let me drop it. And for that reason, I click the link to the news story about Jasper Blackstone. I start reading about how he used a special clause to dissolve the entire board of directors at BFE. According to a bylaw, he has seven days to replace each member, or previous members could resume their seats. He also fired sixteen executives, all of whom had previously burdened the company with sexual harassment lawsuits that were settled in arbitration. My heart flutters as I read a direct quote from Jasper, who states that he vows to change the culture of BFE. He sounds like a man who has no intentions of abandoning the family business. Then he mentions his fiancée, Julia Valentine, will be taking over as vice president of communications.

I feel as if a solid ball of cement has formed in my stomach as I read on. Jasper went on to say that he and Julia have been dating for nearly a year and that they plan to marry in the spring.

I close my eyes, take a deep breath, and press a hand over my queasy belly. I could throw up. And just like that, the pain of rejection rises to the surface. My tears fall. My sobs begin slowly, and then increase in intensity. There's a lesson to be learned. However, at the moment, I have no idea what it is, but I know it exists.

A jolt of reality hits me. I sit on the side of the bed, realizing it's time to be the person I was before I became involved with Jasper Blackstone. I thought he could be trusted, but I was wrong. I force myself to stand up and smile.

I will not be defeated.

First, I order dinner through room service, an Angus beef burger and garden salad. I finally check my voice mail, no longer hoping Jasper has called to beg for forgiveness. Most calls are from editors wanting to know what I've been working on lately or they're pitching stories of interest they want me to look into. Three of the messages are a moment of silence before the call ends. For some reason, I feel Jasper on the other end of the silence, or maybe I'm still wishful thinking.

My ex-boss, Rachel Givens, has called four times. "I have an offer you can't refuse. Call me," she says in her first message.

"Holly, why haven't you returned my call?" she sings in her second message. "Call me."

The next two are in the same vein as the first two.

Hearing her voice makes me smile and firmly grounds me in the life I had before allowing Jasper Blackstone to ruin it. I decide to call Rachel first thing in the morning. I feel like my old self after room service drops off dinner. I eat, do some preliminary research on a few possible articles to pitch to Rachel when we speak tomorrow, and then bathe. Hours later, I crawl into bed perfectly relaxed. I finally fall asleep with Jasper Blackstone on my mind.

***

THE MORNING WENT BY FAST. MY ALARM PLAYED "The Star-Spangled Banner," one of my favorite rise-and-shine theme songs when I'm working. I made a cup of coffee in the hotel's K-Cup coffee maker. It tasted terrible, so I picked up another cup of coffee at the Starbucks in the lobby along with a breakfast sandwich and two bottles of water before hitting the road.

That was two hours ago, and now I'm staring

at a small house in Chattanooga, Tennessee. The dwelling reminds me of one of many hovels my parents moved us into years ago. Snow collects heavily on a weak roof. Dead trees brush up against a rusted fence. Just for a moment, I see my eight-year-old self shivering on the old porch, happy to freeze my ass off rather than be inside with my parents yelling at each other about not having enough money and how it's all my father's fault.

It doesn't look like anyone lives in the house. Black film covers the windows, so I can't tell if the lights are on inside. The day is gray and dark so lights should be on inside. Kylie was right. The house is abandoned. But perhaps I can get inside and take a look around.

"Let's get to it, Holls," I mutter and grab my coat. It's time to rally.

Bundle up, readying myself to mingle with the cold. I step one foot out of the vehicle, careful not to slip on melting snow.

I walk carefully to the front gate and push it open, moving the snow out of the way. The sidewalk hasn't been shoveled. My feet sank into the snow as I make my way to the front door and knock just to make sure no one lives here.

"Can I help you?" a female voice calls from behind.

I jump, startled, and then quickly turn to see a stout woman standing between my vehicle and the gate.

Yes... Someone to collect some information has just shown up. I head toward her. "A family named the Greers used to live here."

The woman nods almost imperceptibly. "But they don't live there anymore, thank the Lord. Why? Is one of them in trouble or something?"

My thoughtful grunt is silent. *In trouble?* I smile at her now that we were face-to-face. However, she's still frowning as if she doesn't trust me on one hand and is waiting to hear some news about the Greers on the other.

"Not that I'm aware of," I say. "I just have a few questions for them."

"Are you a police officer?"

I shake my head. "An investigator."

Her eyes narrow as she studies me more intensely.

I press my hand over my heart. "By the way, I'm Holly Henderson."

She hesitates. "I'm Nel Banks."

My hands are getting cold, so I shove them into my coat pockets. "Did you know the Greers?"

"Not personally. They were strange people. The girls were always in and out of the house, but they never talked to anyone in the neighborhood."

That's a red flag. "Oh, then they were loners?" I ask.

"Very much so. But my daughter used to have some dealings with one of the girls."

Excitement races through me. I thought I would have to do more legwork to find out more about the family who used to live in the house. *But could Nel Banks be my golden goose?*

"Oh yeah?" I say. "Do you think your daughter will mind talking to me about the Greer girl?"

Nel narrows an eye suspiciously. "I don't want my daughter to get caught up in any trouble."

I look her in the eyes and show her my most trustworthy expression. "I promise you that won't happen. I'm a journalist. I won't print her name. I just want to know if she could point me in the right direction."

She grunts thoughtfully. "You want her to be a deep background source."

I grin from ear to ear, impressed she knows how

to speak the language of my trade. "Yes. That's exactly right."

Her body seems to relax some. "Well… Alexia, my daughter, doesn't live here anymore. She used to be in the dark, but now she's found the light." Nel must've read my expression because she explains, "Drugs."

"Oh." I nod. "Good for her."

"Yes indeed." The hard-earned memories of going through hell with an addicted child moisten her eyes. "Today, she works as a librarian in New York City."

I know the genuine warmth in my heart is reflected in my smile. "That's nice to hear. Congratulations." I turn to glare at the house the Greers used to live in. "I know what the darkness feels like." A chill runs over me, and it isn't because of the cold.

NEL BANKS INVITES ME INTO HER HOUSE SO THAT she could make a phone call to her daughter, Alexia. She's a divorced woman who makes a home with three cats. She offers me coffee, but I tell her I'm down to one cup a day, which I've already had.

It's almost the truth. I don't drink as much as I used to, but two is my max. However, I never drink a beverage prepared by anyone when I'm working. One never knows what might be put inside the liquid. However, the more comfortable Nel becomes with me, the more she reveals about the Greers. For instance, she would only see the girls and a man she assumed who was their father, but never a mother. Sometimes, the father would pull up into the driveway late at night with only one girl in the car. Often, it appeared as though no one was home at all. The Greers had an intimidating way about them, which made it easy for them to keep to themselves.

"Nobody wanted to bother them," Nel says.

She also reveals that she learned years after Alexia's sobriety that her daughter used to meet one of the daughters in the woods to get high. Nel has never asked her daughter to elaborate, because drugs were a thing of Alexia's past, and she hadn't wanted to stir old memories or cravings. However, she believes Alexia is strong enough to talk about the past today.

"Sometimes she volunteers at treatment programs to mentor young girls who battle addiction," Nel says before placing a call to Alexia, who agrees to speak to me in person. It was Tuesday, so I'll travel to New York City where we plan to meet on Thursday in the East Village, near the library in which she works.

Nel and I wrap up our encounter. It's good to know that my trip to Chattanooga hasn't left me empty handed. As soon as I hop into the SUV my cellphone rings. I'm not expecting for it to be Jasper. It just doesn't feel like the right time of day to receive a call from him.

I turn on the engine, and the call is immediately transferred from my phone to my car's system. The name comes across the screen. I was right. It isn't Jasper. It's Rachel my old boss.

"HEY RACH," I SAY AS I FINISH STRAPPING myself in.

"What's wrong with you? You never put me off like this. Four calls, Holls. And now you've forced me to make a fifth. I'll forgive you if you make it worth my while."

I laugh softly, knowing that she's only have kidding. "Sorry about blowing you off. What can I say—I've been busy."

"Oh." She sounds highly curious. "You're working on something new?"

"Nothing major," I say, downplaying what can possibly be the seeds for the sort of story that could ruin the Blackstones' reputation forever.

"All right, keep it to yourself, then. Listen…" I picture her big bright eyes widening more with excitement.

"I'm listening."

"I have a new job."

"Oh yeah? Do tell."

"I'm the executive producer of a new show called *Deep Source Real News*."

"Okay…" I say rather impatiently as I perform an Internet search on my phone to see whether or not the airport has a drop-off for my rental. Instead of driving all the way back to Philadelphia, I decide to fly instead.

"It'll be two one-hour shows every night on BCN. I'm hiring fifteen of the top journalists in the country to deliver current and thoroughly investigated news. No story will go unchecked, and every story will have several sources. And you, my darling, are going to be one of my lead reporters."

I smile, not because of her haphazard offer but because I find a drop off location for my vehicle.

"Ah…" I scrunch one side of my face. "I'm not interested in TV. You know that."

"But you have a face and figure for TV."

I roll my eyes as I drive away from the curb and carefully head to the airport. "That sounds superficial."

"You have the brains too. You're tough, humble, and respected. Viewers will come back night after night to eat you up."

"Wow, Rach, thanks. You don't hand out those sorts of compliments often. But it sounds like you want to make me a television host." I know I sound just as offended as I feel.

"No, I don't give out those sorts of compliments often, and no, I don't want to make you into a television host."

"Then why does my face and figure matter?"

"You'll appear on camera as—"

"Ugh," I picture how those sorts of news shows went on BCN. "The talking heads, the opposing positions arguing for the sake of argument, and the overly emotional host who discusses shit that should appall us all with a slight smirk—it's not that kind of show, is it?"

"Oh God, Holly. Why do you make shit so difficult? Do you really think I'll produce that kind of garbage? Especially at a time such as this? I'm making real news for TV, tried and tested and all from the best journalists in the world."

"I don't know," I say, even though I suddenly find myself slightly interested.

"It pays well."

"How well?" I ask before realizing it.

She tells me the figure, and my mouth falls open. "What? Really?"

"That's the kind of cash television has to offer."

Suddenly, another face comes to mind, one I haven't conjured for the longest time. It's that of my father, Harper Henderson. He's in prison, but after being released, he will be sure to look for me. If I'm on TV every day, he will know exactly where to find me.

When I lived in Boston, I received a phone call out of nowhere from a loan shark threatening to break my father's neck if he didn't pay the fifteen thousand dollars he owed. I was forced to use most of the money I had saved for my first real vacation. It was going to be a gift to myself. I didn't even know my father was in Boston, but it seemed like he got into new trouble every month. I bailed him out of jail more times than I could count. When he got sloppy drunk, I would hightail it across town and over to the bar to take care of him. I had never brought him back to my place, though. Instead, I'd put him up in a hotel.

As far as I know, my father has no idea I live in Philadelphia. He hates the city, which was why I was shocked to find him living in Boston. But New York is the city of all cities. Maybe, just maybe, he'll keep out of the Big Apple.

"Holls? Are you still there?" Rachel asks.

I clear my throat. "Yes, I am."

"Is your hesitation about your father?" She knows all about my issues with Harper.

"Yes." The tightness in my throat makes me barely audible.

"You can't run from him forever."

I groan. "Why not?"

"Because you're not fifteen anymore."

"I know," I say as the Navigator tells me which street to turn down next.

"Plus, I have a story you might be interested in. You're friends with Bryn Blackstone, aren't you?"

I sit up straight, pinching my back against the seat. "Yes. Have they found her?"

"No, not yet, but this is about the whole shebang."

I frown. "The whole shebang?"

"Ah, ah, ah…" she says as if scolding me. "I can't tell you what I know until you sign my contract."

I sigh anxiously. "But TV? Are you for real, Rach?"

"You know it's your next big step, Holls. Listen, come to New York and let me woo you."

"Woo me?" I laugh softly.

"Woo you. At least give me a chance to convince you to say yes."

I sigh again.

"How about tomorrow at ten?" she asks.

I focus on the trees and snow melting on perfectly manicured fields of winter-brown grass as I drive up the highway. The hustle and bustle of New York City seems millions of miles away. I planned to make a trip to the city to see Alexia, but that's two days away. However, I like the idea of keeping busy, moving forward, and not sitting still to cry over Jasper.

"Okay," I finally say. "I'll let you woo me."

———

DROPPING OFF THE RENTAL CAR AND PURCHASING A ticket to fly home went smoothly. After landing at

Philadelphia International Airport, I called an Uber. Now I'm standing in my living room, relieved to be surrounded by my things. But also, something lingers in the air. I can't quite put a finger on what, but it feels as though someone has been in my place recently. My glower falls on my furniture then on the big, wide windows, which are the reason I purchased the apartment. I always keep them open, whether I'm home or not, but I scurry over to pull them close.

I pad into my kitchen and look around. The counters are still clean, and so is the floor. The refrigerator looks undisturbed, but I open it just in case. Everything seems to be how I left it. Then I turn to my bedroom.

My heart nearly beats out of my chest. I feel the tiny hairs standing up on my neck. I quietly fish my pepper spray out of the drawer near the oven and take my baseball bat out of the pantry.

I realize I could be totally crazy and imagining things right now, but it's better to be safe than sorry. Slowly, I tiptoe out of the kitchen and down the hallway, opening the closets, creeping into the hall bathroom, the guest bedroom, and then my bedroom. After I clear my master bathroom, I realized I'm definitely alone in my flat.

I sigh. What a relief. Why am I so paranoid these days? Then Arthur Valentine's beady eyes, deep with evil, come to mind. I'm scared of him, and I know why. I love the man who is obligated to marry his daughter, and getting in the middle of Jasper and Julia's relationship is a very stupid thing to do, and a very dangerous thing too.

Woo Me

HOLLY HENDERSON

efore bed, Rachel sent my travel itinerary. A limousine arrives at my row house at seven a.m. sharp and drives me to the airport. Fresh orange juice, coffee, and bagels with cream cheese are waiting for me in the back seat. As far as wooing goes, Rachel is starting off on the right foot.

My one-hour flight to New York lands at LaGuardia less than an hour later. There's a brisk pace to the morning that I welcome. Not since yesterday have I thought about Jasper Blackstone. My brain fought the urge to do so up until I'm sitting in my second limousine of the day, drinking a mimosa and eating chocolate-covered strawberries, pineapple, and apple slices. My cell phone rings, and I answer it, thinking it's Rachel calling to check on me.

"You're doing well," I say.

"Who's doing well?" Jasper replies in his customary grumpy voice.

I gasp, which makes a piece of strawberry and chocolate go down the wrong pipe. Embarrassingly, I end up coughing uncontrollably.

"Jasper?" I finally ask after I calm down enough to speak.

"If you're coughing, don't talk. I can wait," he says.

His tone makes me want to shrink in my seat. I feel like a schoolkid being scolded by a parent. This is not how I pictured my first conversation with Jasper post making love to him and then finding out he's in a public relationship with Julia. The strawberry down the wrong pipe has somehow taken the wind out of my sails. I clear my throat one last time. "I'm fine," I say even though I still sound strained. "What do you want?" I wish I could have sound harsher.

"What are you doing in New York? We didn't discuss you being in the city."

I shake my head as if I had just been zapped by

a jolt of electricity. *I mean, the audacity of this guy.* "How do you know I'm in New York?"

"Why are you here?" he asserts.

My shock gives way to anger. "Are you serious? You didn't even have the decency to say goodbye before leaving the other morning, and now you're asking me why I'm in New York? Screw you, Jasper. You're arrogant and entitled. Screw you." Those words have been pent up inside me for two days, and I'm thankful for the opportunity to release them, although saying that doesn't make me feel any better.

As usual, Jasper is silent. But I'm not going to expend any energy directing him to say something.

"I apologize for how I handled that situation," he finally says. "I wanted to be more considerate."

What the hell does that even mean? "Situation?" I ask, angrily drawing air quotes.

"You did see that I left you a note?"

"Yes, but——"

"Did you read it?"

"Of course I did," I shout. "Can you imagine how it feels to wake up in the morning, and the person you offered your most intimate parts to is gone?"

"Then you're in the city because you're looking for me?" he asks.

The driver was watching me through the rearview mirror as I laugh bitterly. *This guy…* I point my watery eyes at my lap as I burn with anger, and pain. Without another word, I press the End button on my cell phone. That was impulsive. I immediately regret hanging up on him. But I don't know how to fully process that call we just had. Jasper and I are clearly not on the same page.

Five times Jasper calls, and I send each of his calls to voicemail. However, each time I do that, the dull ache in the pit of my stomach pushes me closer toward answering. But if Jasper thinks I'm one of those desperate girls who will put up with him controlling me while he does whatever he wants to do, then he is wrong. Having the face of a hunky angel and the figure of Adonis carved in marble is the sort of beauty capital that can ruin a man—or woman.

How in the hell does he know I'm in New York anyway?

FINALLY, WE ARRIVE IN MIDTOWN, WHICH I'VE always termed one of the busiest places on earth.

We drive through the maze of tall buildings until we reach the Time Warner Center. Thank goodness I'm in a big, fancy car that commands a lot of respect. My car drives right past the others and a valet makes space for me to be dropped off right in front of the gigantic glass doors. I'm then escorted inside by a smiling doorman who knows to refer to me as Miss Henderson. Rachel is certainly pulling out all the stops. But I'm still not sure TV is the way to go.

The inside of the building is ultramodern and bustling with business. The energy is gripping. I'm soon handed off to a woman named Tori Royal. Tori talks fast and she says she's an associate producer for the show I'll be working on.

"I'm not working on the show," I say but either she doesn't hear me or she doesn't care to hear me.

Tori never stops talking about all the perks of working for the show as she escorts me to a more private elevator. There are free meals in the dining center, which is more like a five-star restaurant. The gym comes with my own trainer to keep me on track with a healthy workout regime for when I'm on and off the road.

"Do you run, Holly?" Her studious gaze runs from my head to my feet then back to my face.

I wonder what's the conclusion of her little assessment of me. Hmm…

"Um, yes, usually," I say. "But I haven't done it in a while." I can blame Jasper for that too if I wanted.

"I can tell. You have a runner's body. The tread-mills are high-end." She goes on about free massages, facials, and sleeping suites on the top floors in case I need to catch a quick nap. All flights will be first-class, and some private. I can book a car to take me to the airport whenever I want.

She would keep listing perks if the elevator doors hadn't opened.

Our attention is completely stolen by Rachel standing in front of us with her arms open wide. "You're here," she sings as she throws her arms out before her.

We hug.

"I am," I say in the same jubilant tone.

Rachel looks the same, with her easy smile, dark-brown hair, and light eyes. My eyes travel up and down her thin frame. She's wearing an expensive black pantsuit that makes her look like the boss that she is. "Will I have to dress like this every day?" I ask.

"No, no, no," she scolds. "Don't start searching

for a reason to bail out on me now. First"—she slaps her hands together—"did you enjoy your rides to and from the airport?"

I smile at the light in her eyes. She's purposely going to make it difficult for me to say no.

"Yes, I did." Except the last part when Jasper Blackstone called to hound me about being in the city.

"Good. Now, how about we get down to business?"

"The sooner the better," I say and follow her into another elevator.

———

RACHEL TAKES ME ON A TOUR OF THE NEWSROOM, including the editing bays. She reveals that I will spend most of my time on the road. But she explains how I will work from a satellite truck with an editor and a producer who will be sitting in the editing bays where we were standing. It's the place where they will build my news story for the broadcast.

"Exciting, huh?" she asks but doesn't wait for me to answer.

Truthfully, it's sort of exciting, actually.

"We'll give you one to five days to have your story ready," she says with a glint of passion for her profession in her eyes.

Then she introduces me to a team composed of a field director named Tabatha, a cameraman named Luke, a lighting guy named Richard, and an audio tech named Scott.

"You'll also have two field producers, who are really good," Rachel says.

Every time I shake a hand and introduce myself to capable team members, it becomes harder to tell Rachel that I will have to pass on her offer. The operation is impressive but I can't give up my autonomy so easily.

Then we enter a nice office with an off-white leather sofa and two high-backed black velvet chairs. A big desk is right in front of the window, which has a stellar view of Central Park.

I compliment her posh work space while noticing the floating wall shelves, which hold a few trinkets. "You haven't done much decorating, though."

Rachel points her hand at the executive's chair. "You sit there."

I grimace, suspiciously. "Why?"

"Just sit," she urges, her high-pitched and

cheery tone, giving her away. She sits in the chair across from the big chair.

I sigh reluctantly, but do as she asks. "I'm still not convinced," I say.

"Well…" She sits back in her chair and folds her arms. "This job is also going to come with the story that's going to take your career to the next level."

Then I remember the carrot she dangled. "Right. You have something on the Blackstones."

She smiles coyly. "On BFE."

"So spill it," I say very fast to get her to blurt what she's keeping from me. It's a tactic and I very much doubt it will work on Rachel, but still I tried.

"Uh, uh, uh." She shakes her head. "If you're going to follow this story, then you're going to do it for us."

I shrug indifferently. "Either I'll take your job offer or do it as a one-off. But you know I want to remain a hard-news investigative reporter with my reputation still intact, so this story better be worth it."

She rolls her eyes. "You don't lose your cred because you're doing TV, Holly."

"I do not concur."

"Burt Glass contributes to the Peterman News Hour just about every night."

Passion makes me thrust myself forward. "Right, and I don't believe a damn thing he says. I want to know his goddamn sources."

"You'll have a team. A big, beautiful team that's going to help you dig deeper and faster. Plus, I've hired the best researchers and fact-checkers on the planet." She shakes her finger at me. "And you know better than to doubt it if I say it."

I bob my head from side to side, letting her know that I agree. "True." I twist my mouth as I ponder her offer. I can't deny that I'm excited about working with a team that will help me investigate stories. I've been doing that all by myself, and in many cases four or more sets of eyes and ears are better than two sets. Plus, I'm between research assistants. I've never been good at hiring them. But Rachel knows how to find diamonds in the rough, which was how she unearthed me.

"Okay, I have one foot in the door. You'll have to divulge your lead on the Blackstones to get my second foot over that threshold," I say.

Rachel's eyes slowly narrow to slits as she studies me scrupulously. "You promise to not take our lead and run if you don't end up taking the job?"

"I promise," I say, making sure my tone is sincere. Plus, Rachel knows I'll never screw her over.

Then, as if commanding my full attention, she leans toward me and I feel how sacred whatever she's going to say will be. "The sexual impropriety that's been going on in that company is on a scale the world has never seen. I'm talking about with-holding paychecks until women sleep with their bosses in actual sex dungeons. Assistants are cajoled into prostitution for clients and their bosses. They've only hired female assistants. Six of the male execu-tives are registered sex offenders. And I heard that the rabbit hole runs deeper than that." Her eyes are wide and she's looking at me as if what she told me is definitely the story of the century.

I almost forgot to breathe while listening to her. Part of me wants to run out and ask Jasper if he knows anything about what Rachel is claiming. Another part of me knows that Rachel has to have proof that even an inkling of the story is true before she sends me out to investigate it. But I have to be honest with her before she agrees to assign me the story.

I stare at the door as if I have to make sure it's appropriately sealed. "I have something to tell you."

She turns her head curiously, wearing a curious frown, and that gives me leeway to speak.

My mouth feels too dry to speak plainly, so I swallow to moisten it. "I've been involved with Jasper Blackstone."

She nods and her expression remains unfazed as though what I just told her is no big thing.

That's not like Rachel at all. "You already know, don't you?" I ask, eyeing her curiously.

Rachel smiles wryly. "Kylie Neeland is the host."

I throw my hands up as if I'm done. "I can't believe her."

Rachel rolls her eyes hard. "Oh come on, Holls. Off with the dramatics. We need to break this story, and if you're close to Jasper Blackstone, you're probably the only person who can stay ahead of him."

My neck juts forward. "What do you mean, stay ahead of him?"

"I don't think he's involved, but he's been sweeping his father's and maybe his brothers' shit under the rug since before he graduated from college. I say that to let you know that he's formidable. We need to prove this story before the guy they call Ace goes into cleanup mode."

I nibble nervously on my bottom lip. Does she know how serious it's been between Jasper and I? *Should I tell her?* I think it's my journalistic duty to say something.

She shrugs her eyebrows twice. "Come on, Holls. You can do it."

I grit my teeth and groan. "I don't know, Rach. He's impossible, and I don't ever want to see him again. Plus, he's marrying Julia Valentine."

Rachel sighs. "I heard. But their relationship doesn't ring true to me. And I'll tell you why. She was in love with a guy named Octavio Soto, a polo player from Argentina. About six months ago, he was found nearly beaten to death in an alley near Thirty-Fourth. After that, their relationship ended. My sources say that her father, Arthur Valentine, actually ordered the poor guy's murder because he opposed their relationship. She's a beautiful girl, and her father always has his eyes on the—" Rachel gasps as she put a hand over her mouth. "Holy grail, Jasper intends to make her First Lady of the United States of America." She sounds like she's just been struck by illumination.

I close my eyes, forcing myself not to cry as I nod. "I know." Of course Rachel would figure out their intentions in a snap. She's savvy in that way.

She knows how people like the Blackstones and Valentines think and act.

"Wow, you really like him a lot. I'm sorry, Holls, but men like Jasper Blackstone…"

I open my eyes, happy that I staved off the tears. "Have obligations. I know."

She continues looking at me with sympathy. "Listen, don't worry, I can put someone else on the story."

"No," I say abruptly. "I'll do it, and I'll take the job."

Rachel's eyes grow wide with excitement. "You will?"

My smile is genuine even though it feels forced. I'm experiencing a strange paradox. I don't want any other reporter to handle the investigation into BFE. I also want to prove to myself that I can investigate the family without feeling guilty about it.

"Why not?" I say. "You were right. It's time I take that huge next step into the next stage of my career."

"Yes," Rachel shouts as she pumps her fist. It's odd because she's not at all acknowledging my hesitancy. "I promise you, this is the best decision you've ever made. You're my last hire. Tonight, I'm going to introduce our entire team at the Gold Star Gala."

My jaw drops. "Gold Star Gala? I didn't bring anything to wear to a gala."

"This is New York. We can get what you need like"—she snaps her fingers—"that."

Suddenly, I'm blinking slowly in disbelief. "Wow. Did I just accept a new job?"

Rachel rises to her feet. "Yes, and this is your new office." She extends a hand.

My eyes take in every aspect of my surroundings. "Ah… You tricked me," I say, laughing.

She grins wryly. "Catch." I open my hands as she tosses me the keys to my new office. "By the way, I knew you would say yes."

Foreplay

HOLLY HENDERSON

I check into my home-living suite at Park Royale Hotel. I don't pay a dime. The show will foot the bill for the first three months, after that I can choose to live there permanently at a reduced rate of $8,000 per month—*yikes*—or move. I think I'll move.

Kylie calls as soon as I set my coat and purse on the sofa. We plan to meet for a late lunch in the hotel's restaurant after my appointment with Louis Ramsey, the fashion designer. Rachel's assistant has arranged for him to dress me for tonight's gala.

Ramsey arrives before I'm off the phone with Kylie. He and his assistants roll in six racks and four bins full of dresses, accessories, and shoes for me to choose from. It feels like a tedious situation. I'm

89

done with the special treatment, and truthfully, after the day I've had, all I want is to be at home in Philadelphia, in my pajamas, while working on my next story, which does not involve Jasper Blackstone. *I mean, what was I thinking, accepting this story?* I need to run away from the Blackstones not scoot closer to them.

I select a long, sleek golden gown made of silk with a sexy low-hanging cowl neckline and spaghetti straps. The material hugs my curves with a sultry ease. The first thing that comes to mind while checking myself out in the mirror is that Jasper would love to see me in this dress. I miss him. And I shouldn't miss a man like that.

I let Louis and his team select my jewelry, cocktail purse, coat, and shoes. I say yes to all of their suggestions because let's face it, they know more than I do about fashion. Hell, I would be fine going to the gala in a pair of jeans and a sweater. But nevertheless, leaving my look up to the professionals has served me well. My head-to-toe look is pretty stunning, but I say no to hair and makeup. No more poking and prodding, I have that late lunch to prepare for.

Finally, Ramsey and his team roll out of my suite the same way they had rolled in. But less than a minute later, just as I flop wearily on top of the bed, there's a knock at the door.

"Here I come," I call, looking around to see if Ramsey has left something behind. Nope, he's taken everything. I figure it's Kylie, who's probably starving like I am and is ready to eat now.

I make a mistake. I don't check the peephole before opening the door. This is New York City, I should always check to see who's at my door before opening it. But it's too late and when my eyes meet Jasper's, my jaw drops.

"Hello, Holly," he says. His tone is all business.

My heart constricts and my gaze deepens so much that it feels like I'm falling into him. His scent is like dew drifting on my skin. And he looks delicious in a pair of black slacks and a black crew-neck sweater under a gray ski jacket. His hypnotic eyes watch me with intensity. Then he blinks and that one act, releases me from being under his control.

I swallow the knot in my throat. "What are you doing here?"

He glances nervously across his left shoulder. "Are you going to let me in?"

I would never say no to Jasper if he's standing in front of me and gazing into my eyes. After a shivering sigh, I step back and gave him space to enter.

I close the door and so fast I'm in his arms. His hard body is against mine. My back is pressed against the wood. Jasper's delicious tongue is in my mouth, and his lips feverishly devour mine.

His hands on me…

His taste…

His scent…

I am melting.

"Don't ever talk to me like that again," he whispers thickly while kissing me and pressing his full erection against my hood.

"Don't you ever talk to me like that," I say breathlessly.

In a hazy daze I simper as one of his eyes narrow playfully and he smirks.

Suddenly, I'm off my feet and I'm being cradled then carried. I am savoring every bit of our mouth-watering kiss. We're in the bedroom. I'm on top of the bed. Jasper pulls the belt of my fluffy white robe and when it falls open, he sucks air at the sight of my body. I' m wearing a white tank dress. The material is thin and soft.

"You're so sexy," he whispers lustfully.

I squirm under the full force of the need projecting from his intense eyes. Jasper's soft and warm palm is against my belly, sliding up to cup one of my breasts. He sucks air between his teeth as he squeezes my flesh and then the nipple. My body quickens as I sigh with pleasure.

"I want you," he declares.

Just look at his bulge. Yes, he wants me. His hand slips under the skirt of my lounge dress, fingers slide under the crotch of my panties, and when he touches my wetness, Jasper verifies that I want him too.

"Umm," I say, licking my bottom lip.

"Shit," he whispers thickly.

This is the moment, the final step before entering the point of no return.

"Wait," I sigh, capturing his wrist with both hands and then very quickly rolling off the bed and onto my feet. My head feels woozy. "No." I can hardly take my eyes off his magnificent bulge. But I have to get a grip. We can't keep using sex to mitigate the many issues that exist in our relationship or lack thereof.

But Jasper is on the move. He's now standing in front of me. His warm breath cradles my face. "I miss you."

I resist the urge to sink into the palm of his hand. I'm angry at him and I can't let his intoxicating touch and presence make me forget it. "That's your fault, not mine," I hiss.

"Damn it, Holly. I apologized for hurting you."

"It seems you're always having to apologize for hurting me, Jasper. When I don't want to be hurt at all."

"That's not true, and you know it."

I shake my head. "I haven't even known you a month, and the hurts you've made me feel aren't small ones, Jasper. They're huge, heart-torturing hurts."

His shoulders collapse when he sighs. "You know our circumstances aren't normal."

I close my eyes and say, "I know. But I still think you're intending to marry Julia."

"I'm not marrying her."

"I don't think you have a choice in the matter as far as Valentine's concerned."

"Babe," he whispers fervently. I'm in his arms again. "You have to stop worrying about him."

There's something in his eyes that I haven't seen until now. I have no idea how to name it. Only, I believe him, and Arthur Valentine is a bad man. So what does that make Jasper?

"Why does everyone believe you're damaged and dangerous?" I blurt.

His body goes rigid. "Who believes that?"

I question whether or not I should've mentioned Rachel's assessment of him. However, I haven't been able to get her words out of my head. She would never make such claims without proof.

"Many of my colleagues. The ones who don't make those sorts of accusations without evidence."

His gorgeous eyes soften some as they search my face. "Do you believe I'm damaged and dangerous?"

I shrug. "I don't know. You would have to be if you have no fear of Arthur Valentine."

Jasper snorts bitterly. "He's a bully, Holly. And as far as he's concerned, I am dangerous. And the damaged part"—he shrugs—"maybe."

I inhale sharply as my lips part. Am I revolted by him? Turned on? More in love with him because yet again he told the truth?

"But I will never hurt you, Holly. I will die before I do that."

My eyes close as I allow lightheadedness to pass. I want to stand in his arms, just like this, forever. But still... I think it's best to wait until he handles his Valentine problem. "I can't," I whisper.

"You can, baby." He kisses me. It's a soft tender kiss that makes my heart flutter. "Yes, you can."

"No, I can't." My voice comes out in a whimper...a helpless whimper.

Jasper stands very still, and for that reason, I open my eyes. His gaze holds mine captive.

"Holly, listen to me and listen to me good. I know how to be Randolph Blackstone. I was given that lesson from day one. But I rejected my father and his ways. As a boy, I harbored nothing but pain, anger, and resentment for him. He gave me a harsh education. He called it the Roman way." He snorts, snarling. "I could've been just like him, but I had made a conscious effort to be different. And I am different. But I'm also better than he ever was."

Jasper's level of introspection holds me spellbound, turns me on, and makes my heart want to jump out of my chest to melt with his. I swallow the lump in my throat and throw my arms around his neck. We make out feverishly. All I feel for him is raw desire. A thought comes to mind. I try to banish it. Now is not the time to say it, but what's on my mind wants to find its way out regardless.

"Jasper…" I whisper and suck air, feeling the tickling sensation of his lips and tongue on my neck.

Now is not the time, Holly.

He grinds me hard with his hard cock. "What is it, baby?"

Oh God… the pressure of his hardness against my sex stirs a pleasurable sensation. My desire is so high, I forget what I have to say. Then I picture myself sitting down with Rachel earlier and now I remember.

"Jasper, I have to tell you…"

Knock, knock, knock.

The sound brings me back to earth.

"They'll go away," Jasper whispers before his mouth consumes mine again.

"But I'm supposed to have lunch with Kylie," I whisper. Then I call, "Who is it?"

"Hi, Holly Henderson. It's me, Rod Huff," the man says.

My eyes grow wide.

Jasper gives me a who's-that look.

"Rod Huff?" I croak. Oh… Now I remember. He's a man I had sex with a few years ago during a journalism conference in Denver… or it could've been Seattle. No, it was Chicago.

"Who is Rod Huff?" Jasper whispers, pronouncing every word sharply.

"A colleague."

"I'm sorry. Are you busy?" Rod calls.

"Tell him to go away."

My eyes narrow to slits. I don't think I will ever

get used to Jasper ordering me around, which means if he wants our relationship to flourish, he'll have to work on that annoying habit of his. However, in this case, he's right.

"I'm not decent at the moment. Could we talk later?" I ask.

Jasper is shaking his head. I look away from him to better ignore him.

"Umm…" After a pause he asks, "You'll be at the gala tonight?"

Jasper's jealous glare is burning me alive. "Yes," I call.

"How about we get together beforehand? We can ride over together."

"No," Jasper whispers.

"Um…" I'm terribly confused.

"I can meet you in the lobby at eight," Rod says.

I squeeze my eyes tight. I don't want Rod escorting me to the gala, but I don't want to obey Jasper either. "Okay."

"Great. See you then." Rod sounds ecstatic about our eventual meeting.

Jasper and I stand still, staring each other in the eyes. Why in the world do I feel as if I'm cheating on him? I'm not. He's not my boyfriend, and I'm certainly not his girlfriend.

Jasper arches an eyebrow. "You're stubborn. You know that?"

I crack a smile. "I resent being called stubborn."

"Then stop being stubborn."

"You can't order me around, Mr. Blackstone."

The sexual tension between us is fierce.

Jasper tips his head curiously. "What is this gala you're referring to?"

I fold my arms defiantly. "I'm surprised you don't know anything about the gala. You knew I was in New York. You also knew I was here. Are you the one paying someone to follow me?"

"Yes," he answers without the slightest hesitation.

My mouth falls open, "Why are you having me followed?"

"You really don't know the answer to that?"

Our lips are so close that I wish he will kiss me. "Yes, I know it. Valentine," I whisper.

"He knows you're in Manhattan and believes you're here for me."

"But I'm not here for you."

A flash of desire brightens his eyes. "No?"

I shake my head. "I have a new job."

"Job?"

"A news show on BCN…" I shake my head out of frustration because I can't remember the name of it.

"I see," his voice is sexy and smooth like butter. "Where's the gala?"

I feel as if the tone of his voice has just injected me with obedience serum.

"I don't know," I say. "A car is supposed to take me to the event. I never asked for the address, but it's the Gold Star Gala."

He nods softly.

His delicious breath spreads across my face and I'm still waiting for him to kiss me. But then I remember the allegations against BFE. Now is the time to say something about my new assignment. However, he takes a step back, leaving my lips lonely.

"Um, Jasper. I—"

My cell phone chimes, and I look over at the phone, which sits on the nightstand. It must be Kylie.

"Damn it," I say under my breath. "I'm late."

"Late for what?"

"Lunch with Kylie."

"Kylie Neeland?"

I turn impatiently towards the chiming. "Yes."

I'm torn between answering the call and enlightening Jasper about the allegations against his company. He's already walking toward the door.

"Where are you going?" I ask.

"We'll talk soon," he replies and walks out of the room.

The phone becomes quiet.

"Damn it." I rush to the console to call Kylie back. I frown at the number of the missed call. It's an unknown number with a local area code. Since Jasper is more than likely long gone, I listen to the message.

Alexia said you were asking about me. She won't meet you. Please call me and tell me what you want. You have my number.

It's her.

My fingers poke eagerly at the numbers on the screen. My nerves stand on edge as I wait for the woman to answer. After the fourth ring, the call goes to voice mail. I frown. She should have picked up since she left me the message not even a minute ago.

"Hi, it's me, Holly Henderson." Since she's playing coy, I get right to the point. "Does the name

Randolph Blackstone ring a bell? Please let me know. I'll be waiting for your call."

My phone rings shortly after I hang up.

"Hello," I answer eagerly.

"Holly, where the hell are you? You're late," Kylie says.

Pinching the bridge of my nose, I restrain a sigh. And then I hear a beep. *Damn that's her.* "Sorry, Kylie. I'll be downstairs shortly," I say in a rush.

"How short is shortly?"

"Less than five minutes."

"The clock is ticking."

I end our call and look at my screen. The previous caller has texted me. *Please do not call me again. Go away. Leave me alone.*

"Shit!" I shout loud enough to release my anguish.

I'm shaking for so many reasons—Jasper, the unknown caller, and Kylie. I must calm down. I jump into a pair of black cigarette pants, a cream cable-knit sweater, and riding boots. I grab my purse and room key and head to the restaurant for our late lunch.

As I slip into a crowded elevator, I picture Gina's face as she gave me the lead on the house in Chattanooga. There was something in her eyes. She knew something. I didn't see it then, but I see it now. Only as the elevator carries me up several floors to the penthouse restaurant does it occur to me that she was giving me a solid lead born out of real knowledge. Truthfully, I thought for sure that Kylie would find the address led to a low-rate brothel—but not so. Things are heating up. I want to know why the mystery woman had such an extreme reaction at the mention of Randolph Blackstone. I kick myself for how I played my last communication to her. I made a mistake. I shouldn't have mentioned him until we were face-to-face.

"Damn it, Holls," I mutter as the doors open at the floor I want.

People look at me but I don't care. Damn it, indeed. If only I could walk away from learning the mystery woman's connection to Randolph Black-stone. But now, I'm more determined than ever to find out her name and her connection to the dead man.

The Colleague

❦

HOLLY HENDERSON

Kylie snaps her fingers. "Woo-hoo, earth to Holly. Where are you?"

She and I are at a table for two. I ordered the classic Italian Bolognese. *I'm starving.* And she...

I refocus on her face. "Sorry..." I massage my temples. "I'm just so tired. It's been a long day."

The truth is, I can't get my correspondence with the mystery woman and Jasper off my mind. On top of that, I'm thinking about Bryn.

"So..." Kylie rubs her hands together. "What did you find in Chattanooga?"

I raise my eyebrows, remembering Kylie always has an agenda. I suspect she's still hell-bent on destroying the Blackstones, which means our interests are not aligned.

I shrug. "No one lives at the address."

She twists her mouth thoughtfully. "Is that so? I did see a skinny guy wearing an oversized coat go inside."

I hold a bite of my Bolognese in front of my lips as I think. I believe Nel when she said no one lives in the house. I wonder if Kylie is telling me the truth and if not, then why is she lying to me?

"It could be a trap house," I say and then explain my encounter with Nel.

Kylie's eyes gleam with excitement. "Now you're talking. So, what's next?"

Ah… I see. She's trying to keep me interested in the story.

I don't mention Alexia and her friend, the mystery woman. I'm not ready to reveal that to her yet, or maybe I won't tell her at all.

"Nothing's next, Kylie. I'm waiting for another lead to fall into my lap."

"That's bullshit and you know it," she snaps.

I remain unruffled as I casually take another bite of pasta. "I don't know what you want me to say or do."

She shakes her head continuously, watching me chew. "This is not the kind of reporter you are,

Holls. You don't want to know more because you have feelings for Jasper Blackstone. Admit it."

If only that were true. I actually *want* to know more because I have feelings for Jasper. I want to know everything about what makes him the man I'm falling in love with. But, as I chase down what I've just swallowed with a drink of water, I realize that I have to throw Kylie off my trail.

"What about Bryn Blackstone?" I ask. "I've been out of the loop for a few days. Do you know if the authorities are close to finding her?"

Kylie looks at me with wide eyes. I can see her brain processing my question behind them. I asked her the right question. If I would've asked her about anything or anyone else other than a Blackstone family member, she would be lambasting me right now for purposely changing the subject.

"Nothing yet." She actually sounds sympathetic.

It feels like a good time to reveal a secret to her. I check over both shoulders then lean across the table. "Did you know she's supposed to marry Carlton Valentine?"

At first, she frowns as if she doesn't recognize the name. Then her eyes grow wide. "Oh, *the* Carlton Valentine? Arthur Valentine's son?"

I nod, paying attention to all of her major and minor reactions.

"But she was…" Kylie turns her head slightly. "Jasper is…"

I smile smugly, knowing I have just helped her put the pieces together.

"The Valentines are trying to regain the political power they lost in the nineties?" she asks.

"It seems so."

"Shit, Holls, then that's why Bryn hired you. I racked my brain, trying to figure out a logical reason why. She wants you to destroy her family."

I nod. "I've thought that too."

"But do you believe it?" she asks.

I fold my arms. "Maybe."

"Well, we're very close to doing just that. That's if you don't sell us out." She's watching every bit of my reaction to what she just said.

"What do you suppose I do, Kylie? Huh? Go right to him and question him about the allegations against executives at BFE?"

Kylie shakes her hands in frustration. "Be the goddamn reporter I know you to be, Holly. Gosh, you know what to do. You're the best at getting what you need without asking direct questions.

Please bring that Holly to the table and not this subpar journalist."

I roll my eyes indifferently even though her statement cuts me to the core. She's right. The mistake I'd made with the mystery woman earlier was not like me at all. I even left Nel's house too quickly. Deep down, I believe she knows more about the people who lived across the street than she was willing to admit. Maybe they were scary people. So yes, Kylie is right. I'm better at my job than I have been in recent days.

"I'm sorry, Holls. I didn't mean to insult you," Kylie finally says.

Suddenly, I realize I've been gazing at her unfocused with watery eyes. I shake my head. "It's okay."

"Listen, I would have Rachel take you off this story, but you're the only person who can keep us in front of it. But here's what I want to know. Are you really able to blindside Jasper Blackstone?"

"Blindside?" I ask. I never said anything about blindsiding Jasper.

"How else are you going to make him be honest?"

Frowning, I shake my head at her. Now I see it.

I've heard it in her voice over the phone but now, I can actually see it.

"Why are you so insistent on taking down the Blackstones? Surely this isn't all about your ego," I say.

Kylie sits up straight and spreads her fingers over her collar bone. "My ego?" Either she's offended or clueless.

I nod curtly. "Yes. Your ego."

She watches me, blinking as I wait for an answer. The seconds tick by, and that's when I see something a lot clearer than I had before this very moment. She's willing to do whatever it takes to bring down the Blackstones, Jasper in particular, even if that means using me up to get what she wants, and then leaving me to pick up all the pieces of what will be my shattered relationship and possibly career in her wake.

No Fire for An Old Flame

HOLLY HENDERSON

K ylie and I remember that we are friends, and I mostly listen as she talks about moving to New York, how she and Rachel initially pitched the new show to the executives at BCN, and the highs and lows of that period in their lives. She's still single and the pickings are slim in the city. She says maybe I could be her wingwoman, and she could be mine. I don't respond to that comment. She's fishing. Although I should respond to throw her off my track. But I don't. Before we part ways, she assures me that she and I will be seated at the same table tonight along with other members of our investigative team. The thought of sitting with other reporters who are part of the show makes my decision to work at BCN feel more real. I'm actually going into TV. *Is this what I want? Why am I so afraid of the change?*

Then there's Jasper… I don't know what to do about Jasper. At the moment, I can't visualize a world where we are together, loving each other without being hindered by one thing or another. He's definitely not on the up-and-up. Will I have to betray my profession just to be his girlfriend, or even better, his wife?

I make it back to my suite, I try calling the mystery woman's number but receive a recording telling me that the number is no longer in service. I follow up with a call to Alexia and receive the same recording.

"What the hell," I whisper as I drop down onto the sofa with a long sigh.

The plot has just thickened, making me more determined than ever to figure out the story. Due to the sloppy way I handled my trip to Chattanooga, I forgot to ask for Nel's phone number. But I'm not certain if Nel would be up to helping me at this point. I'm also certain that Alexia contacted her mother and let her know that she did not appreciate hearing from a strange reporter about her mysterious friend. My mind races as I try to figure out what to do next. But the gala starts soon. I have to let go of the investigation for the night, so I scuttle to the bathroom to brush my teeth.

My cell phone rings, and I dart into the bedroom to answer it. I cross my fingers, hoping the caller is the mystery woman or even Alexia, but it's Rod Huff informing me that I'm eleven minutes late for meeting him in the lobby at eight p.m.

I quickly pull the phone away from my ear and look at the time on the screen. My mouth falls open as the time turns to 8:12 p.m. right before my eyes. Damn it, I forgot all about meeting him in the lobby.

I gush with apologies and tell Rod I'll be downstairs in less than fifteen minutes after admitting that time has gotten away from me.

"Working on a story?" he asks.

"Yes," I say.

"Then you're excused. Take your time."

I smile. Now I remember why I came to know Rod. He's a good guy, and from what I remember, handsome too. But we never shared anything close to the same chemistry that I have with Jasper. He liked me. I liked him. However, the more time we spent together, the more I learned that Rod and I just weren't meant to be. Regardless, I would be excited to hang out with him tonight if I never would've met Jasper Blackstone.

I take a quick shower, slide into the gorgeous dress I tried on earlier, apply a light coat of makeup, and use styling products to sweep my noncompliant hair into a back bun while leaving soft hairs cascading along the sides of my face. A final glance in the mirror nearly takes my breath away. I look stunning, if I may say so myself.

My mind betrays me as it pictures Jasper ceremoniously loosening my hair and sweeping my tresses to one side so that he can fervently but delicately taste my neck.

"Stop, Holly," I sigh then took a deep breath. *When am I going to stop craving that man?*

Needing to shake a tail feather, I rush into the living room and grab the cocktail purse that matches my dress off the sofa. Next, I pluck my room key off the coffee table, stop in front of the door then look around to make sure I hadn't left anything.

"My coat!" I run as fast as I can into the bedroom and carefully free the gold trench coat that matches my dress from a hanger. I put it on, but I still feel as if I'm missing something even though I have everything I need.

I FEEL LIKE A BALL OF MESS WHEN I SEE ROD IN THE lobby. His eyes raise from his cell phone to me. By the way his gaze devours me, I'm pretty sure I look better than how I feel. Apparently, I'm getting more attention than I expected, not only from my old friend, who's escorting me to the gala, but from whomever else I pass. *See what a little makeup and an expensive dress can do, Holls?*

Closing the rest of the distance between Rod and me, I smile at him, and he smiles back. He's still tall, blond, and in good physical condition. The dimple on his chin still makes him look like a movie star. It's obvious two and a half years has done him well, being that he looks more like a man. I think he's thirty, or thirty-one—he's close to Jasper's age.

"Wow," he says when I reach him. "You look beautiful."

We hug.

"So do you," I say as we let go of each other.

Rod boldly curls an arm around my waist. "We should go."

I'm mildly taken aback by the ease with which he makes such an intimate gesture. He's sort of claiming. I wonder how Jasper would feel about the way we're walking side-by-side, looking like the perfect city-chic couple. He wouldn't like it. No, he would hate it.

However, I feel obligated to allow Rod the freedom to make us appear as if we are a real couple. After all, I'm almost forty-five minutes late, which I apologize for again.

He tightens his hold on me as we make our way through the lobby.

"It's no big deal," he says. "I'm just glad to be with you."

I look at him with wide eyes, hoping he means that in a way in which two people are friends and not lovers.

As soon as my face hits the cold, I put Rod's last comment out of my mind. A chilly wind nearly freezes my face off. I hug myself tightly as Rod guides us to our limousine. Then, like the gentleman that he is, he takes off his coat and lays it over mine, giving me an extra layer of warmth.

"Oh no, you don't have to do that," I say, postured to give him his coat back.

"I insist. I'm from Alaska. The cold is going to have to do better than this to get to me."

We chuckle. I forgot how charming he is. If only Jasper could be so amiable. Rod even takes the driver's place and holds the back door open for me.

"Thanks," I say as I slide into the back seat of the limo.

"My pleasure." His tone is flirty, and so is the way he's looking at me with raised eyebrows.

I feel confused. Shouldn't I let myself enjoy a night out with a handsome man? I don't have a boyfriend. I smile at Rod as he slides into the back seat with me. He was clearly happy to see me.

"So, how have you been, Holly?" he asks, flashing that winning smile of his.

The car pulls away from the curb.

"I've been well," I say because it's the customary reply. "And you?"

He smiles. "I'm well. You really do look beautiful tonight."

I blush because of the way he's watching me. There's a sweetness to it. When Jasper gazes at me, I usually see something intense in his eyes. His gaze is completely laced with fire and desire. *Umm...* It's as though the simple fact that he wants me so much makes him angry. As long as I live, I will never be able to fully figure out Jasper Blackstone. He's the abyss, the dark sea, and buried in his depths are treasures—wonderful, beautiful treasures.

I squeeze my eyes shut to banish Jasper out of my head. I can't do this all night, think about him, and then try not to think about it. It's pure torture.

"Is everything okay?" Rod asks.

Shit... I stop scrunching my face and smile brightly. "Yes, and thank you." I point my hand at him. "You look handsome too."

Rod tosses his head back and laughs as though I had said something terribly entertaining. That's when I realize he's very nervous. We have history, and I've tried not to think about it, but now I accept that his goal is definitely to rekindle our past, which didn't end on the best note.

When we met at the conference in Chicago, we had sat next to each other during the first panel of the day. There was an ease between us as we made comments under our breath when the silly girl from *Outlast* magazine tried to sell us on using search engines to churn out more articles. Halfway through her talk, which had been dispensed in a mind-numbing Valley-girl accent, Rod looked over both shoulders and asked out loud, "Is this for real?"

I was the only one who laughed out loud. We decided to accompany each other to the next panel, which was just as asinine as the first. By the third, I realized we had attended a conference for bloggers. Our companies picked up the tab, which included room and board, so we decided to stay and make a good time of it.

Even then, I regarded him as someone who was especially handsome. Ken dolls were based upon men who resembled him, even though he wore a little scruff on the lower part of his face and had windblown blond hair. The wilder parts of his appearance didn't seem natural. It was as though he was attempting to shed his all-American-boy image.

I can't remember if we engaged in a deep conversation, but I do recall that he complimented me a lot on my looks. And the more he gushed about my looks, the less authentic he became in my eyes. But he was fun. And he talked a lot about how much I would love Alaska and how much he missed home. He asked questions about me too. I couldn't recall them, but I remember that every time I answered, I felt as though I were failing the "my first wife" test.

By the end of the night, we went to my room for drinks. One thing led to another, and we started kissing. Then we engaged in the most awkward sex ever. I remember saying "ouch" a lot. He directed me left and right. He spent most of the night trying to keep his cock from softening. And he assured me that it wasn't me; it was him. I really didn't care who it was. I had already chalked our mishap up to a severe lack of sexual chemistry.

As I sit in the back seat of the limousine with him now, I wonder if he remembers that night. I'm surprised it hasn't turned him off so much that he never wants to see me again. I guess there's no better cure for a bad experience than time.

"By the way," I say after a question drops out of the blue and into my head. "How did you know I was staying at the hotel, let alone my room number?"

Rod keeps his eyes cast down as he grins. "I saw you at the counter checking in earlier." Then he abruptly shifts in his seat. "Hey, I wanted to congratulate you on *The Howsley Project* and *In Defense of Bad Air*. Two times out of the gate, you hit all the major best-seller lists."

I smile graciously. "Thanks."

"So, are you seeing anyone?"

I feel a pinch of discomfort because I didn't expect him to ask that question. Of course, Jasper's face, kiss and touch come to mind. "Nope." I said that way too optimistically for it to be true.

Rod grunts, intrigued. "I can't believe you're

still single." He might've as well said, "I can't believe my luck."

For some reason, I feel as if I should mention Jasper to him in some way, shape or form. "Well, I just got out of a relationship," I add. "A hot but short one."

Shit, now the lust is back in his eyes.

"He was a lucky man. Remember the night we tried to have sex?" he asks.

Laughing awkwardly, I want to run and hide. "I do."

Rod smirks. "I'm more experienced now."

I smile at him, realizing he's implying he wants a do over. "Aren't we all?" I manage to say. But I don't like how suggestive that sounded. "I mean, experienced in everything. I'm a better journalist than I used to be. I'm now a reporter for this new show on BCN. I mean, it's TV. Never in a million years did I think I'd be doing TV."

Rod smiles weakly, and I can see his disappointment as he gazes at me. At least he got the message. I had expertly steered us away from any talk of a sex do over. There's no way that's happening.

His posture is a lot looser. "Oh, we're part of the same show."

My eyebrows flash up. *Interesting.* "Finally, we're colleagues."

He smirks. "Maybe we can have lunch or dinner together soon."

"What about you?" I ask with gusto in an effort to change the subject.

He frowns. "What about me?"

"Do you have a girlfriend? Wife?"

Rod scoffs. "No wife. I had a girlfriend. She's crazy."

I smile tightly although I've learned that it's best to avoid men who describe their exes as "crazy." That usually means he's the one who drove her crazy. "Aren't they all?" My tone is cynical.

He appears irritated. "Aren't they all? What do you mean by that?"

I shrug timidly. Apparently my little, and very bad joke, has gone over his head. "Ex-girlfriends."

He shrugged indifferently. "It takes two."

"Ah… Then you're crazy too?"

He frowns as if he's not understanding the exchange we're having. But I know he understands perfectly. He's just pouting, but I continue to play along.

"You said your ex was crazy, and then you said it takes two. So…"

"I see," he sighs.

Thank goodness our car stops in front of the Guggenheim, the venue for the gala. The hoopla of our colleagues getting out of vehicles and walking into the circular structure being followed by photographers with flashing cameras steal my attention.

"Are you nervous?" I ask my eyes shining while I rub my hands together.

I turn to Rod. He's still looking as if he's pouting. "It's just a gala."

Thankfully, the driver opens my door. I scoot out in a rush. For some strange reason, I feel free and want to get as far away from Rod as I can. Time speeds up after our feet hit the cement and we start mingling with colleagues we hadn't seen in ages. It's as if I've stepped into a time machine. By the time I make it to the red carpet to take my photo, Rod and I have lost each other, and that's a relief.

Our Show

HOLLY HENDERSON

The main event is being held in the tastefully decorated rotunda room. Round tables are covered by light blue silk tablecloths, and blocky centerpieces made of clear glass are lit by silver candles which are inside of each. The table settings are elegant white porcelain with shiny silverware and crystal drinking glasses. Waiters serve us white or red wine. I know better than to mix the two, or else my stomach and head will pay for it later, so I drink the red.

But oh gosh… The excitement in the air cannot be contained. I am having a lovely time already. Kylie has managed to seat me beside her. Seated at our table are Rachel and her husband, Matt; Daniel Arroyo, who is a journalist's journalist; Dave Eastman, the actual president of BCN, and his wife; plus Katherine Donovan, a woman who owns a number of news stations in the country. Rod takes a seat on the opposite side of the table next to two empty chairs. I try to make eye contact so that I can smile at him to send a message that we're still on good terms within the friend zone. He won't look at me.

Kylie, who has been going on about how much of a success the night is shaping up to be, suddenly hits me on the arm. "What's he doing here?"

I follow the direction of her scowl, which is pointed at Rod.

"Rod Huff?" I ask in a high-pitched voice.

She squeezes my arm and quietly shushes me.

I'm baffled by her response to him being here. "Isn't he one of the reporters for *Deep Source*?"

Her jaw drops, but then she picks it up and aims a glare that can freeze molten lava at Rachel. "He wasn't supposed to be hired." Her eyes are still fixed on Rachel, who was obviously avoiding looking in our direction.

"Why not?" I ask.

She shakes her head. "He's my ex."

I force my face to not show my surprise. *But oh*

my stars. Was Kylie the crazy ex-girlfriend Rod mentioned in the car.

I'm about to let her know Rod and I rode to the gala together but my attention is quickly stolen by a couple who sits in those two empty seats between David Eastman and Rod.

It's Jasper and we can't seem to take our eyes off each other. He's with a date, a gorgeous, raven-haired beauty, the same woman who confronted Jasper with her father on the morning I left the Blackstone mansion in tears. He's out tonight with Julia Valentine. The sight of them together, looking like the perfect couple, makes my insides feel as if they're coiling into knots.

Kylie slaps me with her knee as tears pool in my eyes. "Did you invite him?" she whispers, her mouth close to my ear.

I shake my head.

"Damn it," she mutters. "Then he must be Dave's guest." She and Rachel finally make eye contact. Their expressions communicate what their voices can't at the moment. If Jasper and Dave are friends, then broadcasting a story regarding sexual misconduct at BFE won't be easy.

At the moment, I don't give a damn about their investigation. I'm trapped between wanting to get up and storm away from the table and remain seated to really get an idea of how close Jasper and Julia truly are.

"*In Defense of Bad Air* and *The Howsley Project*," someone says to my left.

Only now do I realize I'm staring at Julia—when I'm forced to look away from her. I should not be jealous. I don't think I've been jealous of another woman in my life. Now I know how it feels.

I turn to Daniel Arroyo smiling at me, and the tone of his voice said he appreciates my work. I should be excited. It's my moment to shine. Daniel's one of the best journalists on the planet and he's just called out my books.

But still, I have to force a smile while coaching myself to pull it together. "Mr. Arroyo, thank you." I don't know him well enough to call him Daniel, but I'm hoping for the invitation to do so.

"It's Daniel," he says, and just like that, my smile turns real. "There aren't many young reporters like you willing to put in the sort of legwork you did, go to the places you went. That was great journalism, Miss Henderson."

I can't believe Daniel Arroyo has just praised my journalism skills. Now my head feels floaty because of that as well. But I keep my composure and press my hand over my chest. "It's Holly. And thanks again. I truly appreciate you acknowledging my work."

"Daniel, it's great to see you again," Jasper says.

Daniel nods at me and then turns to Jasper. "You too, Jasper. And I send you my condolences about your father."

Jasper nods stiffly. "Thank you."

"So, Jasper, when are you going to announce your bid?" Daniel asks.

Jasper snorts and then abruptly extends his arm across the back of Julia's seat, and smiles. She turns to look at whatever has captured Jasper's attention. They both lean closer and then smile as a camera's flash brightens the table.

Kylie groans her disapproval.

Without acknowledging how aghast I look, Jasper removes his arm from the back of Julia's chair. "Bid? What bid?"

Daniel laughs softly as he readjusts in his seat. "You know what bid I'm referring to."

"Mr. Blackstone," Kylie blurts like she can't contain herself any longer. "I'm surprised you're here tonight. It's sort of brave of you to venture amongst so many reporters."

What Jasper does is very subtle yet potent. He

smoothly allows his gaze to pass over Kylie while showing no expression whatsoever as he turns to Rod. "I'm sorry, have we met?"

Rod jerks his head back surprised Jasper is speaking to him. "Um, I'm pretty sure we haven't."

Jasper grunts thoughtfully. "I saw you with Miss Henderson earlier." He glares at Rod, who seems to be waiting for him to say something else.

"Why are you so concerned with Holly Henderson? Aren't you marrying your fiancée?" Kylie blurts, smirking at Julia.

Julia glares at Kylie but I see it on her lips—a microscopic smile. Then she rolls her eyes at Kylie and stares at the stage as if she's not effected at all by Kylie's taunt.

"Jasper has made a generous donation to tonight's cause," Dave says, as if the tension at the table has escaped his notice, which I'm sure it hasn't. Dave is too sharp not to detect it.

"Oh, I've done more than that," Jasper teases, wearing a sexy, lopsided grin that captures the attention of all the women at the table except his date.

Julia Valentine seems to be here, yet not present. She's wearing an expression similar to the one she had on Christmas morning. I still can't help but wonder if her somber demeanor is an act, or a tactic.

"Do tell," Mrs. Eastman says.

"Not yet, honey," Dave replies.

Jasper's gaze lands on me again, and Kylie pinches my thigh under the table. "Why does he keep eye-banging you?" she whispers, with her mouth close to my ear. "He has no shame."

"Oh, by the way, Holly, let me know when you're ready to leave," Rod says. Then he sets his attention on Kylie. "We came together."

I gasp and quickly turn to her. "He came to my room and asked if I wanted to come here together. I said yes, but…" I shake my head.

Kylie snarls. "Why do you think I care?"

"So, Holly Henderson," Jasper says as he puts a hand on Dave Eastman's shoulder. There's something about the way he's looking at me. I think I'm finally about to learn why he's here. "We were talking earlier about how talented you are."

Dave springs to life. It's like he's been waiting to have the conversation Jasper started. "Yes, you're so accomplished to be so young."

"You're a beautiful woman," Jasper says, still eye banging me. "You're smart, charismatic. I want to talk to you about having your own show."

"What?" Kylie and Rachel ask at the same time.

"How are *you* calling shots for BCN?" Kylie hisses. The hate she has for Jasper Blackstone is written all over her face.

Dave Eastman and his wife seem stunned by the tone Kylie has taken.

"Kylie meant…" Rachel starts. Her skin is red and blotchy. I don't think she knows what to say. After all, she's onboard with Kylie's plan to shed a negative light on Jasper's business. But as of tonight that plan looks as if it's going up in smoke.

I figure I better say something. "Sorry Mr. Blackstone…"

"Jasper," he quickly corrects.

"Jasper," I say. There's a moment of pause and in this moment it feels as if he and I are the only two people at the table, in the world. His smirk is making me forget to breathe. I've also forgotten what I was going to say until this very second. "Um, Jasper, Kylie was just…"

He raises a hand to stop me from talking and it works. "No need to defend Miss Neeland. She and I have history. It seems we've battled our rounds. She's the cat; I'm the mouse. Or am I the tiger, and you're the rodent?" Jasper winks at her, grinning as if he's just joking. But I know him. Jasper doesn't joke. He's fucking with her. And I think it's so damn sexy.

Kylie thrusts herself forward, casting her energy at Jasper as if it's an electrical rod. "Oh no, you're certainly the tiger, but one day, you will get caught, skinned, and worn like last year's Gucci."

I press my fingers against my lips. *Shit, did she just say that to Jasper Blackstone?* Luckily for her, Jasper is grinning with amusement rather than spite.

But Dave glares at Kylie as if he's been ready to fire her ten seconds ago. "Watch yourself, Miss Neeland."

Jasper puts his hand on Dave's shoulder again, it's a I-have-all-the-power touch. "Please don't hold our banter against us, Dave. Miss Neeland holds truth to power. BCN needs her. Plus, she's hosting our new show."

My jaw drops. "Our?"

Rachel's eyes expand. "Our?"

Kylie jerks herself back in her chair. "Our?"

Snakes and a Angel

JASPER BLACKSTONE

I like seeing Holly in her element, among her colleagues. She has a controlled way of engaging with the table and processing the scene. I can see why Bryn asked her to dig into our family, and how she has outwitted me on several occasions. For the most part, her beautiful face only gives what she wants away. However, she can't keep her eyes off Julia. I can see that she's feeling as if she's not my first choice. *Holly baby, you're always my first choice.* This is not a date Julia and I are on.

Earlier, after Holly mentioned the gala, I recalled how Stephanie, my personal assistant, informed me about my invite to the event. I initially declined the invitation, especially since I'm at the tail-end of negotiating the purchase of BCN. It's best these sorts of deals are kept silent for as long as possible. I didn't want our competitors, like Kathy Donovan to have access to me until the deal was done. But here I am because of her. And I hadn't meant to mention my purchase of BCN tonight, but I slipped. I let Neeland get under my skin. Score one for her. And the reason why Julia is here is because she'd convinced me to use tonight as an opportunity to make her father believe that her and I have a real connection. I agreed even though I'm close to having both Valentines out of my way soon.

My eyes spark with amusement as I watch Holly. *So this is how she looks when she's jealous?* How long can I resist her? She has the poise and shrewdness that her colleagues seated around the table lack. It's easy to subvert Kylie Neeland. She's a spoiled brat who feels as if she has permission to blowup the world in the course of getting what she wants. I could bring her career to a grinding halt if I choose, especially after that stunt she pulled with the coroner's office. She's lucky Holly's on her side. It would only take one phone call to initiate her free-fall—just one.

"Mr. Blackstone, any word on your sister?" Rachel Givens asks.

The question comes out of nowhere and Givens

looks smug, not at all concerned about Bryn. I glance at Holly, and she appears ready to hear the answer too, it seems the whole table wants to hear what I have to say. Even Julia, who's leaned closer to me. But she's closed some distance between us only because Holly's watching.

My frown makes my temples ache. "Is what you're asking on or off the record, Miss Givens?"

Givens slyly glances at Neeland—they're both conspiring to give me a hard time.

"It's neither on or off the record," Dave says with an awkward laugh as he readjusts in his seat. "There'll be no journalism tonight. This is a celebration."

Neeland has her mouth ready to say something.

"At least he could tell us why he decided to buy one of the biggest media companies in the world," Kathy Donovan says, beating Neeland to the punch.

I smirk at Kathy because she's smirking at me. *We're going to do this in front of the journalists, huh?* She's put together a conglomeration in hopes of killing my deal and snapping up the station with her team of buyers. Good luck with that. Her effort is an impossible long shot. I can't lose this deal, and I won't lose it.

Victoria mutter's something about being bored. I scratch my neck out of irritation. How in the hell could she be bored at a table that's as live as this one? Here we sit in a den of snakes, the scene is hot, and she's too self-absorbed to see it.

I avoid Holly's eyes, though. I can feel her curiously waiting for me to answer Kathy's question. I'll speak to her alone about my purchase of BCN later on tonight. *And I will see her later on tonight.*

"I could ask you the same question," I say to Kathy.

Kathy has a habit of making a high-pitched humming sound when she's on a roll. She makes the noise, and then says, "You came in out of nowhere to crush the little people."

My shoulders shake as a laugh escapes me. She's playing to the table. "When did you become 'the little people,' Kath?" I called her Kath just to let the table know how her and I run in the same circles.

Kathy stretches her lips into a cunning grin. She's called me out in front of Holly, and now I'm forced to explain myself.

I clear my throat and steal a glance at Holly, who's still watching me. *Fuck.* She's not happy.

"Plus," I continue. "BFE was interested in BCN

four months ago when we learned, as I'm sure you did as well, Kathy, that the company has been operating in the red and going under steadily and surely." I take another quick look at Holly. Her frown has eased some. *That's a relief.*

Julia's long sigh is audible. She sounds like one of those puffed-up women who has nothing to do on a hot day but lay around and try not to absorb too much heat. But I can't take my eyes off Holly whose expression has just become very unreadable.

"Is that so?" Kathy says. "Because it seems sort of impulsive from where I'm sitting."

"Kathy, when have you known me to be impulsive?"

Kathy watches me with one eye tapered as she rubs the side of her neck. I'm done engaging with her. My response was meant for the ears of one person and one person only. I face Holly. Her soft lips part. I want to kiss them.

I only look away from my object of desire when Givens stands abruptly. "I have to go to the ladies' room." She zeroes in on her colleagues. "Kylie, Holly, would you like to join me?"

My heart races as I watch Holly rise to her feet. I want her to stay put, but she looks down, breaking our eye contact and excuses herself from the table.

They all walk away together. Holly's body looks tantalizing in the gold dress she's wearing. I briefly fantasize about slowly, ceremoniously, peeling her out of the silky material. *I can hardly wait.*

Dave asks Kathy a question about the health of one of the smaller stations she owns. During a pause, I turn to see Kathy open her mouth as if she's going to say something. She doesn't want to answer that question in front of me. I could say something sly, like "Go for it, Kath. I already know you're running your stations into the ground." But I wouldn't dare—not in front of Dave and Daniel.

Then Kath says, "Oh, sorry, Dave," and tells him she just received a call she's been waiting for while showing him her cell phone.

"Business never sleeps," she says as she excuses herself then walks away from the table with her cell phone against her ear.

Now that she's gone, I figure there's no time better than the present to learn why the guy sitting to my left knocked on Holly's door this afternoon and asked her to be his date for the evening.

I fold my arms on my chest. "So, Rod, tell me about yourself."

Rod grins from ear to ear like he's happy my

attention landed on him. "What do you want to know?"

I take a swig of champagne. "How long have you known Miss Henderson?"

He frowns.

Shit. The mistakes I'm making tonight continue to mount. I should've asked him to tell me about himself first and then inquired about his relationship with Holly.

"Why are you asking?" he says still looking disappointed.

"You don't have an answer?" I ask, figuring there's no turning back now.

He holds my gaze for a moment. "I met her about two years ago at a conference."

I grunt thoughtfully, nodding. "You must've liked her."

"Yeah…" He shrugs as if his interest in Holly is no big thing. "She's beautiful. Sexy, actually, but she's not into me."

"I'm going to the restroom," Julia announces and shoots to her feet.

Feeling the wind that she stirs as she storms off, Rob and I look at her go.

"That's Julia Valentine, isn't it?" he asks, keeping his gaze pinned to her back.

"Yes." I don't know why it pains me to say that, but it does.

"You're a couple?" he asks after Julia disappears into the same hallway that swallowed-up the other ladies.

"She's my vice president of communications." I keep a straight face, looking him in the eye, hoping that answer suffices.

Rod grunts thoughtfully. It looks as if he's about to ask another question but I realize I have to beat him to the punch, stir our chat in the right direction.

"I heard you're part of a new show on BCN. Congratulations," I say.

Rod sits up straight. The look in his eyes says he has Julia off the brain. "Yeah… And you too. You own the outfit."

I snort, smirking. "Almost."

"It sounds like a done deal to me."

I wink at him to let him know he's on the right track.

He suddenly leans forward like a fisherman who just got a bite on his hook. "You're going on the record."

I chuckle. "About what?"

"Ah…" He says nodding. "Can I get first dibs?"

"JBlackstone at BFE," I say, giving him my email address.

He relaxes in his seat, nodding smug. "Thank you," he says as if he's relishing in his victory.

Rod manages to pull me into a conversation about best practices when it comes to running a corporation as large as BCN. I smirk, listening to Rod subtly give me input on how to run the company. I like input and he has some good ideas. Through my peripheral vision, I keep an eye on the hallway the ladies entered. I can't wait to see Holly again. I want to watch her walk to me. Maybe I can figure out a way to get her alone before the evening ends. I want to kiss her. I lick my lips thinking about how I need to kiss her.

I've zoned out on Rod who hasn't stopped talking yet. Thankfully, a voice comes over the PA system, telling us dinner is about to be served, and then a petite woman named Lisa Barrington talks about the purpose of tonight's gala.

I peer deeper into the hallway. Holly, Kylie, and Rachel have been gone longer than I'm comfortable with. However, Rod wants to resume our conversation. The guy is definitely a talker. While Lisa Barrington shares statistics on human trafficking,

Rod talks about how the gala could've been planned better.

"Why the hell are they serving food right now? After I eat, especially at this hour, I'll be ready to go to bed," he says.

I pep up when I see one of the women exit the hallway. It's not Holly though. It's Julia. She's approaching rapidly, almost trotting. And her eyes are glued to mine. I would search behind her to see if Holly is on her tail, but there's something in Julia's expression that alarms me. She makes it to her seat and I lean away slightly as she guides her mouth to my ear.

"I have to tell you something I just heard. But we need privacy," she whispers.

I excuse us from the table and Rod watches as I stand up with Julia. He probably thinks I'm banging her. I hate that because then he'll think it's okay to go after Holly, which it isn't. Regardless, Julia and I find a quiet room on one of the upper tiers, and that's where she relays what she just heard by accident.

The End of the Gala

HOLLY HENDERSON

"**G**ot it, Holly," Kylie says. Defiance resides in her eyes and in the way she tightens her mouth.

Gosh, does she hate Jasper that much? I'm beginning to wonder if she hates him because he had ignored her sexual advances at one point in time. Her abhorrence of him is nonsensical. Kylie certainly isn't an ideologue when it comes to holding truth to power. She's only dogmatic about furthering her career. She would be wise to not poke the bear named Jasper Blackstone if she were thinking pragmatically. She'd get further if she made a friend out of him instead of a foe. *So why is taking him down so personal to her?*

"Got it," I say weakly.

Kylie looks like she's chewing on nails as she throws her hands up and faces Rachel. "She's going to screw it up, and we have no time. This story has to come out now."

"Calm down, Kylie," Rachel says in her customary reasonable tone. "We may have to admit defeat on this one."

"Never. And I'm not working for him either."

"What is it with you?" I blurt. "Why do you hate him so much?"

"Because he's a crook, and so is the rest of his family." Kylie is shivering slightly.

Rachel and I widen our eyes at each other. *The rest of his family?* I wonder what she means by that, and I'm about to ask her when Rachel reminds us that we've been gone too long. We decide to table our conversation until our nine a.m. meeting tomorrow morning in Rachel's office. Then we will discuss our Hail Mary tactic to get Jasper to sign off on the story about sexual misconduct in Blackstone Industries.

As soon as we're back to the table, my heart feels as if it has tightened into a tiny ball. Jasper and Julia are gone. Their place settings are clear, and when I ask Rod if he knows where they have gone, he says there was an emergency and they had to go home, and he seemed to look gratified when he added, "together."

FOR THE REST OF THE NIGHT, I STRUGGLE TO KEEP A happy face. I don't want Rachel and Kylie to notice how much power Jasper has over me. Whenever I think about Jasper and Julia skipping out of the gala together like the perfect couple on the cover of *GQ* magazine, my stomach hurts. I barely eat the main course and refused dessert. Of course, whoever made dinner was not even a quarter as good as the chef at the Blackstone mansion. The food tonight is subpar, and I plan to order a late-night BLT with a green salad as soon as I get back to my suite.

After our dessert plates are collected, the *Deep Source* team is introduced, and Rachel gives her speech about her plan to air a six-part special with Daniel Arroyo during our first week on the air.

"Real reporters on the ground in real time," she says. "No talking heads. No actors pretending to be journalists. We're presenting objective and serious news coverage, primetime, five days a week."

Earlier, when we were stowed away in a tiny

room near the bathroom, Rachel asked me a number of times how I felt about Jasper owning BCN. Three times, I insisted I didn't have a problem with it. Of course I'm okay with it, but I'll never let her know that. His decision seems rash and pretty crazy. I heard what he said about starting the process of buying the company four months ago, but I don't believe him. I feel he said that for my ears only.

Finally, the night ends, and we all make our way to our cars and limousines. Not many people stick around to chitchat. Just about every face I pass looks as exhausted or hammered. The hotel isn't that far from the venue, and I decide to walk since I don't want to be confined in the back of the limousine with Kylie's ex-boyfriend. It's strange, though —the two barely said much to each other all night. Rod spoke to Katherine Donovan, Dave, and Daniel for most of the night. He also bragged about engaging in a nice conversation with Jasper Blackstone. He kept saying he's a good fit for BCN, which made Kylie seethe.

"Hey, Holly, wait up," Rod calls just as I step out into the cold night. He rubs up against my side, walking way too close for comfort.

I shift to my left to put some distance between us. "Oh, Rod. You know, I think I'll walk back," I say.

He puts his hand against the small of my back. "No way. It's too dangerous. Come on, let's ride back to the hotel together."

Rod is leading me to the limousine. Only a very small part of me wants to insist on walking. Truth be told, I'm too exhausted and heartbroken to ardently object. I want to crawl into bed as fast as I can and figure out how to quit my new job tomorrow morning during our nine a.m. meeting, citing conflict of interest.

On the ride to the hotel, Rod keeps watching me with flirty eyes and a small smile. He wants to have sex, and I just want him out of my sight.

"How about we have a drink together before bed?" he asks.

"No," I say sharply and instantly regretted my tone. I mean, we are colleagues. There's certainly a more respectful way to refuse him. "I mean I'm sleepy. I just want to go to bed."

He nods, still wearing a grin and a faraway look in his eyes. "The last time we tried to, you know, have sex, it wasn't good, was it?"

My sigh exposes my lack of patience. "No, but only because we don't have sexual chemistry, Rod."

"No, it wasn't that. I just think I had too much to drink that night."

I close my eyes, thinking, I really don't want to get into this right now. Also, I don't like the position I put myself in. I probably should've walked back to the hotel. Frankly, I could use some cool air on my face.

"I'm better at it than what I showed you," he says.

I feel the car stop, and I thank the Almighty that we made it.

I open my door before Rod or the driver are able to get out of the car. "Goodnight, Rod." I hurry out of the back seat and walk so fast through the lobby that I'm practically a streak of lightning. I know Rod is somewhere behind me, intending to catch up. But I got a pretty good head start. I see him through the narrow opening of the elevator doors after I rush inside and hit the close button.

Thank goodness I have a straight shot up to the fortieth floor. My hands are shaking, and nervousness grips me as I keep swiping the key to open my suite wrong.

A tall figure steps behind me, and I nearly froze in place.

"Let me get this for you, baby."

I can break down and cry as a familiar presence washes over me. I let Jasper take the key out of my hand, and after one swipe, we're in my suite.

Skin on Skin

HOLLY HENDERSON

I forget I'm mad at him for buying my new place of employment. The few fantasies I had of me giving him a piece of my mind fade. My body and soul are starved for Jasper.

We stand inside my nicely warmed suite. He just closed the door and locked it and we're gazing into each other's eyes. My heart is racing like it's running the one-hundred meter dash. He's so here, so present. He must've arrived not too long ago. I can feel the cool rising from his black cashmere coat. Gosh, he's such a regal man.

"Hey you," he whispers as he softly strokes one side of my face.

I close my eyes and inhale him as my face rests

into his palm. "Hey." I swallow to loosen my tight throat. "So… You and Julia, huh?"

"That was just for show, and you know it."

I do know it, at least I do now. He's here with me and not with her, so yes…I do know it.

We continue staring at each other while breathing heavily. The longer I look at him, the more grateful I am that he's actually here. Then, suddenly, and passionately our lips collide. I whimper as his tongue devours mine, and mine his. Jasper holds me so close to him that I'm forced to release our kiss to breathe, but due to separation anxiety, the pause doesn't last long. We're at it again.

It seems our kissing will never satiate our desire as my body shivers. Emotion that must be pure love pours through me. My head spins. The flavor of Jasper's mouth makes me more desirous for him. His hand has found its way inside the top of my dress to squeeze one of my succulent breasts.

"Mm…" he moans as he sucks my bottom lip into his warm, soft mouth. "Sweet, baby, you taste sweet."

He continues tasting my lips as if they're the flesh of ripe strawberries.

"Oh," I sigh in a shivering voice.

Jasper moans as his rock-hard erection nudges the lower part of my belly, making promises to soon enter my throbbing sex. My fingers muss his hair, which is soft, a distinct difference from his hard body.

"All night, I wanted to tear this dress off you." His voice is filled with fire and desire. His soft, warm mouth trails sensual kisses down the side of my neck and to my collar bone. I put my hands on the sides of Jasper's head as he sucks my right nipple through the cloth of my silky dress. My nipples are so hard, so sensitive, and he wails like a lost puppy as his mouth shifts from one to the other, back and forth. My sex weeps for him as I push my pelvis against him, giving him hints of what I want him to do to me. It doesn't take long for him to catch my clue, Jasper shoves an arm under my dress, and his fingers plunge into my wetness. In and out, he finger-bangs me as he continues with his tongue, teeth, and lips stimulating my nipples.

I sink against the door, capturing my lower lip between my teeth as I succumb to pleasure.

"Holly?" Rod calls from the hallway.

I gasp softly as Jasper presses his lips against my ear. "Don't answer," he whispers.

There's no way I'm going to do that.

Rod calls me again and Jasper sweeps me into his arms. We kiss feverishly as he carries me into the bedroom. I think Rod says something like "I'm sorry" as Jasper lays me down on the king-sized bed. I'm like a curious and aroused rag doll. Our eye contact depends, my chest rises high and falls low with each breath as he lifts the hem of my dress until the material bunches over my belly.

Jasper rips his eyes away from mine to devour my flower. He sees I wasn't wearing panties. I couldn't. I didn't want show panty lines in that gorgeous dress I was wearing. And so, he wastes no time separating my knees, wrapping his arms around my thighs, and guiding his face toward my slit.

"Damn it, baby," he mutters, then his tongue slides up the skin of my inner thigh, teasing me, tasting me, making me squirm until…

I gasp and suck air as erotic sensations spark through my sex.

"Mm," Jasper whispers as he continues his quest to make me come and come hard.

I writhe, grab handfuls of the comforter, and my breathing grows faster and louder as I come close to orgasm. Jasper must love that I'm loud without caring if Rod is still listening.

And oh my… It hits me. "Ah," I cry out at the top of my lungs as I climax, experiencing the ultimate pleasure.

Jasper rises to his feet. His eyes are dazed, looking as if he's just ingested the best drug ever. I can't take my lidded eyes off him as he takes a condom out of his pocket, rips open the packet, and slides it over his engorged cock.

Our gaze remained locked. I have no apprehension about what was about to come next. Jasper spreads my knees farther apart and slowly, indulgently moves into me. My sex embraces him, swallowing him whole.

OUR SKIN GLISTEN WITH POSTCOITAL SWEAT. JASPER rolls me on top of him. I can hear his heartbeats, smell his citrusy, sandalwood, and sweaty scent. I would be perfectly content to stay like this forever, but that's not feasible and we both knew it.

"What is it you have to convince me to do?" he asks out of the blue.

I frown confused. "What?"

"Julia overheard a conversation you were having with your colleagues at the gala."

I quickly raise my head off his chest. He's watching me as if he asked, how's the weather. My lips part, but I'm lost for words. My first inclination is to maintain the upper hand. But the expectation in his eyes makes me think differently. I can't fool myself any longer. In the war between Rachel and Kylie and the man I can't live without, I'm securely on Jasper's side and had been for a while. So I tell him all about the sexual misconduct allegations and what Kylie and Rachel want me to do as far as using my 'sexual sway' with him to get him to spill the beans.

Jasper lifts his chin to blurt a laugh. "Is that what she called it? 'Sexual sway'?"

I sigh, thinking about that long and strange conversation we had at the gala. "Yeah."

"Well, you definitely have sexual sway with me," he sways, his lips lifted into a mouth-watering smirk.

I trail a finger down the crease in the middle of his chest, "Glad to hear it."

We chuckle together.

"But on a serious note, they are aware that they're on the losing side of the coin, but Kylie is just so unable to let it go."

"What about you?" Jasper asks.

"What about me?"

"Whose side are you on?"

"Yours, always yours."

He closes his eyes as if he relishes the words I've just spoken.

"You have no idea how long I've been wanting to hear you say that." He kisses me delicately. "Know that I'm always on your side."

Once again, my mind races back to my conversation with Rachel and Kylie. I promised not to tip Jasper off until we come up with a strategy during our nine a.m. meeting. I didn't mean it when I agreed to wait.

"So, what are you going to do?" I ask.

He heaves a sigh. "The allegations are true." He closes his eyes and releases another deep breath. "I knew horrible shit happened in the Lower Manhattan office, but it was under my father's watch, not mine. I would've never allowed it."

I stack my hands on top of his solid chest and rest my chin on them. "What happened under your father's watch?"

He studies me curiously. "We're off the record. Nothing you say or I say leaves this room, deal?"

My eyebrows flash up. "Deal."

"My father had his demons. He grew up wealthy but not safe. You know what I mean?"

The look in his eyes says it all. Randolph Blackstone was an abandoned and abused boy.

A lump sits in my throat as a thought comes to my head. "Did you grow up safe?" My heart is beating like crazy. I want him to say yes, that no one had ever hurt him. But of course he's suffered. Jasper Blackstone, the destroying angel with his hard shell that I've barely started to crack is definitely wounded.

"No," he says.

I release the breath I've been holding. Our gazes remain locked. I feel like it's just him and I in this whole world. Then, I move my mouth to his for a soft, sensual kiss. As usual, when I kiss him, my heart expands with emotions. Then, I recall Gina telling me that she tried to service Jasper, but he couldn't get it up.

"Can I ask you something," I say after our lips gently part.

"Yes."

"Did you suffer sexual abuse?"

"No. I was tortured to conform to my father's will."

Frowning, I envision some sort of medieval torture contraption that has lots of sharp metal and leather straps. "Tortured?"

"Physically and emotionally tortured. Randolph called it the Roman way."

"The book?" I say with a start.

Jasper sighs audibly. "Yes. The book."

It's the book I found in the library, the one he slyly took away from me.

"Randolph believed he had to mold me into the ultimate warrior who would do exactly what he demanded, no questions asked, no back-talk." He takes a deep breath.

"Wow," I say moving my lips dramatically.

Jasper looks around the room. I've never seen him appear so vulnerable. His eyes land on the desk. He points his chin at a lifestyle magazine. "I'll get that," he says and kisses me as he rolls me off him. Our locked gazes linger a few beats before he's on his feet.

He opens the magazine to an article about the history of the Empire State Building and shows me all the words on the page. "See this."

I nod vigorously. I miss his body already as he reads the magazine for what feels like ten-seconds. Jasper hands me the magazine, closes his eyes to think, then says, "Find paragraph thirteen, the seventh sentence."

"Okay," I say as I sit with crossed legs on the bed. "Found it."

I listen to him recite that sentence and the rest of the paragraph as if he's reading directly from the publication. But he doesn't stop there, he continues until the end of the page.

My jaw drops and then I close my mouth to swallow. "What? Do you have a photographic memory?" I ask even though I'm sure it has been proven that the phenomenon doesn't truly exist.

His slight smile makes him look more youthful than he ever has. "No. You could do the same if you were forced to practice it, given no food or drink, starved of love and connection, until you were able to do just what I did."

I stop breathing as I process what he just revealed to me. I can hardly believe what he just told me. Who does that to a child? Who's ever endured anything like that? I'm speechless and I'm sad, and all I want to do is wrap Jasper in my arms and hold him.

"My father was an egomaniac, a narcissistic loser." He stops snarling and as he inhales deeply, his shoulders rise higher. "He wanted to prove that the Blackstones were supreme by forcing me to be…" He presses his lips together and shakes his head as if he couldn't find the right adjectives for what he has become. "I've made some mistakes recently. Being right here, right now, is one."

"Being with me is a mistake?" I sound so sad even though I know the answer. Yes, being with me is a mistake as long as Valentine is a thorn in his side.

"My presence here is putting us both in danger, but I'm tired of being away from you."

Finally, I pat the mattress beside me, beckoning him to come back to bed. With stellar posture he walks to the side of the bed and lays down beside me. We enfold our fingers. The sight of his large fingers between my much smaller ones makes me feel safer than I ever have.

Then, as eventual as taking our next inhale, our mouths come together for a soul-rousing kiss.

"I'm sorry you had those awful experiences with your father," I whisper between kisses.

"Don't be," Jasper says, taking over the process, guiding me onto my back. Suddenly, he stops kissing me and stares into my eyes. "I am in love with you, Holly. I don't know why or how it happened, but I'll do anything for you."

"Even buy BCN?" I ask before I realize it.

He grins lazily. "I'll admit that you working there helps make me stick with my decision."

I raise an eyebrow. "Where you planning on not sticking with your decision?"

His eyes are slowly becoming lidded and when he grinds me with a brand new erection I can feel why. "Never. But you still bring value."

My sex is begging for him to enter me. "Did you really start the purchase of BCN four months ago."

"Yes, baby," he whispers.

I gasp, stiffening as his cock, surges through me, and then he holds very still.

"After what you told me about Neeland and Given's plans, the value of my family owning BCN just went through the roof."

"What do you mean?"

"I can control the narrative. And you know"— he starts to move in and out of me—"I'm all about being in control," he says tightly.

He feels so good inside me but still, I'm curious about the next move he's going to make. "So, what are you going to do?"

He holds still. "First, I'm going to do you. Then I'm going to ponder whether or not I'll let your friends have what they want."

I widen my eyes. "What?"

Jasper strokes me slowly and indulgent with his cock. We're making love, kissing and unable to keep our hands off each other.

"You're so beautiful," he keeps repeating as his velvety mouth devours the skin of my neck, my mouth, and my tits. With each passing second, he strokes me deeper, more fervently.

I open my body to Jasper Blackstone and for some reason, and I don't know why, I whisper tightly while clinging to him, "Screw me for your own pleasure, not mine."

He looks confused, but he continues stroking my sex.

"Your pleasure, baby," I reiterate even though I realize he's having trouble processing what I'm saying. I'm being naughty, pushing the line because I know he's reacting strongly to words which sort of escaped me without me realizing the power in them.

Suddenly, Jasper stops cold turkey and now he's out of me. I knew it—it was instinctive—focusing on his own pleasure is something he can't do.

He sits on the edge of the bed, with his face buried in his hands. I rub his back, feeling as if he would shrug away from my touch at any moment.

He doesn't, though, and I refuse to stop touching him, massaging him until he tells me to stop.

"Jasper?" I ask in a delicate voice.

"Yes," he replies uneasily.

"How about I order us something to eat and we just lie here together and be each other's company for the night?"

He turns and gazes at me with glossy eyes. I can tell he wants to cry but can't. I wonder how long his tear ducts have been blocked. Perhaps forever. Instead of asking him if he's ever cried a day in his life, I smile faintly but encouragingly.

"How does a BLT sound?" I ask.

He nods softly.

I kiss the skin on his back then gently rest the side of my face over the spot my lips has just abandoned before calling room service to order two BLTs, french fries, sparkling water, and a bottle of red wine. I also order fried donuts with dipping sauce. We both need comfort food.

After I place the order, Jasper reaches for me and wraps me in his arms. I close my eyes, allowing myself to absorb the feeling of being so close to him, skin on skin.

His Best Side

HOLLY HENDERSON

The alarm on my phone buzzes, and I wake up instantly. Before turning it off, I twist to look behind me. I sigh with relief as my heart expands with glee. Jasper is still in bed with me, curled up on his side, and sleeping. I think about how great the rest of our night was as I turn off my alarm. We talked all about the Howsleys, the family I investigated and "ruined". I mean, I didn't ruin them. They ruined themselves by being dirtier than mud. He already knew almost everything I painstakingly discovered through meticulous investigation. Our comparing notes was akin to foreplay. He had won. I didn't know that James Clyde Howsley, the newest patriarch of the family, was one of three suspects in the death of Christine

Taylor. She's an actress whose body was discovered in the trunk of a limousine on L.A.'s Sunset Boulevard.

That lead us to a discussion about Bryn and holy crap, he told me that I shouldn't worry about Bryn. She's not dead.

My eyes lit up. "Really?" I asked excitedly, even though deep down I knew she was still alive.

He told me yes. "She's just being, Bryn."

"Do you know where she is?"

"Not yet," he answered without pause. I love it when he answers without pause. That means he trusts me.

Then, Jasper admitted something to me that made me laugh my head off. Last night was the first time he's ever eaten a french fry.

"I knew it!" I exclaimed, pointing at him.

I told him how I hid my fast food bag under my car seat on the very first day we met. Then, he confessed that he knew he wanted me when I rolled down the window and charmed him with my friendliness.

"No way," I laughed. "Please don't say you were first attracted to my personality."

He rubbed my thigh before capturing it with his large hand. "They run neck and neck—your beauty and your charm." With that one strong hand he pulled me until I was on my back, and then he moved inside me, making love to me yet again.

I smile at him now. He's mine, and I've fallen in love with him.

I chuckle very quietly. *Look how he sleeps.* He's straight on his back with his hands together, fingers enfolded above his groin as if he's a vampire sleeping in a casket. I've never seen him sleep that way. And he looks perfectly content, undisturbed by demons swimming through his head.

I kiss his cheek and he stirs until he opens one eye and then smiles at me.

"Good morning," I sing, smiling from ear to ear.

I love the smile he's showing me right now. Jasper reaches up to guide me to him.

"What time is it?" he whispers as he big-spoons me.

Ooh, that bulge of his is Ready-Mister-Freddy. "Seven," I whisper craving what's about to come next.

"Shit," he exclaims and sits right up. His body heat abandoning me leaves a cooling sensation on my back. "I have to get to the office." He jumps out of bed like a world class athlete. "But stay put."

"Stay put?" I ask, watching him trot to the bathroom.

I can hear his urine hit the water in the toilet. I sit up and look down at my naked body. I've never been so comfortable being this naked around a man. I would put on something like an oversized T-shirt.

"How did you sleep?" he asks.

"Lovely," I say, remembering how safe it feels to be next to him in bed. "And you."

He appears in the room again, pointing an enormous boner at me. "Lovely. Now," he says, kissing me and guiding me onto my back. "Let's have one for the road."

FIFTEEN MINUTES LATER

While Jasper and I shower together, I tell him about Alexia, the strange phone calls I received from the mystery woman, and how I can't reach Alexia anymore.

"Then heed her warning, and leave it alone. I don't want you putting yourself in unnecessary danger. I'll have my people look into it."

I roll my eyes, suddenly regretting telling him.

His lopsided grin is sexy. "Did you just roll your eyes at me?"

I smirk. "Maybe. Yes."

The water makes our kiss slippery. Then something quite surprising happens. Jasper wraps his arms around me and holds me. The warm water spraying from above pelts us as we remain glued together, falling deeper into the feelings of new love.

Finally, after one last kiss, Jasper turns off the shower, dries off, and we get dressed. While I'm readying my face for the day, Jasper surprisingly calls his assistant and has her bring us breakfast.

"I could've just called room service," I say after hotel staff drops off the order.

"Go take a look," he says as he confidently stands, straightening his cuff link.

I open the fancy frosted-glass containers and see succulent shrimp on grits with poached eggs on top. There are fluffy biscuits with an assortment of jellies and a handwritten note that reads, *Glad to serve you again, Bart.*

I gasp into the palm I slap over my mouth. "You didn't."

He winks, wearing a cocky smile. "Of course I

did. Bart will be making all your meals while you're here."

"But…" I frown, terribly confused. Even though our feelings are strong for each other, we are still sneaking around.

"You don't want Bart to serve you?" he asks with an expression that says he already knows my answer.

I twist my mouth anxiously. "Aren't you worried about Arthur Valentine finding out that you and I are still involved?"

"Not as of this morning," he says.

I jerk my head back. "Why not?"

Jasper gathers me in his stalwart embrace. "Let me worry about Valentine."

I hum, wondering if Rachel and Kylie had been right after all. A little too much sex with me and Jasper has lost his common sense. "How about we worry about him together?"

His soft lips caress mine, and our tongues entangle sensually. "I don't want you worrying about a thing," he says breathlessly.

Shit, he's had done it again, rendered me dumbfounded and unable to form a rational argument against him. I guess I'm not the only one with 'sexual sway'. We stare into each other's eyes, knowing exactly what we both want to do next. Only there's no time.

"Tell me something," he finally says.

I raise my eyebrows. "Tell you what?"

"How did you know?"

"How did I know what?"

His expression is open and vulnerable. "That I'm averse to seeing to my own needs above others'?"

"Ah," I say, tossing my head back. I bring my head back to the upright position. "Because, Jasper, I've been paying attention."

After staring at each other for several seconds, our breaths crashing, our mouths collide. Our teeth clash, but our tongues whirl greedily around each other. My pulse throbs in harmony with his cock. There's no way to stop this train.

Jasper thrusts me on the sofa, pulls off my shoes, tugs off my pants, and snatches off my panties. I spread my legs, opening up for him. Through my lidded gaze, I watch as he unzips and frees his hefty cock. Lust fills his eyes. My eager thighs quiver as he opens them wide enough to fit his body and then sinks his cock into me.

THE COAST IS CLEAR WHEN JASPER LEAVES MY SUITE first. I bounce as I saunter down the hallway. I take an empty elevator to the lobby, buy a cup of coffee in the chic café on the first floor, and walk to the office on foot. I don't know why but I feel safe. I'm not afraid of Arthur Valentine anymore. The safest place in the world is on Jasper's good side. I am on his best side. With every step, I try to find my way back to that long list of stuff I have to do today which reminds me… I text Branson, an investigator that I use from time to time, and ask if he could track down Alexia's friend from the phone number she used to call me with. I doubt he would be able to locate her. Something tells me she used a burner phone, but maybe not. It's barely a minute later when Branson texts me back and says he's on it.

By the time I make it to the BCN building and to Rachel's office, I'm still confused about what to tell them in regard to investigating BFE. In my professional opinion, I don't think the story has two legs. It barely has a toe. The real story about the Blackstones has to do with what I discovered at the Blackstone mansion, and I'm not willing to hand that over to Rachel.

When I walk through the door, Rachel is sitting in the yellow armchair, and Kylie is on the matching sofa. They both look up at me as if I've just caught them in the middle of conspiring against me.

"Well, you look balmy," Kylie says, her gaze hopping all over my face. "And you're late." A small snarl comes to her lips. "How did you sleep? Or did you sleep?"

I shake my head and take a seat next to her on the sofa. "I slept well, and you?"

Kylie scoffs and rolls her eyes.

"Well?" Rachel asks. I could see the worry in her eyes.

"What is it?"

The same look passes between them, the one they had when I first walked in.

"What is it?" I demand to know.

"Our story about misconduct at BFE has been pulled. If we decide to move forward with it, we'll all be dismissed."

"But that's not all," Kylie says.

Rachel throws her a look of warning.

"Okay... What else is it?" I ask, wondering if Rachel has decided to just let me go. I hope so. If my position is terminated, I'll probably call Jasper to let him know that I'm going back to my apartment in Philadelphia for a few says. I cut a tiny smile, realizing that he'll never let me go so easily. And if he fights for me to stay, then I would stay.

"Show her," Kylie demands, crossing her arms. She looks smug, like whatever comes next will wipe this stupid smile off my face.

But still, I want to know. I ruffle my eyebrows. "Show me what?"

A Bad Day

HOLLY HENDERSON

"Where did you get those?" I sound winded.

When I saw the photos of Jasper and Julia in all kinds of lovey-dovey poses, I had to force myself not to hyperventilate.

"They were sent by an anonymous source," Rachel says.

"Bullshit," I retort.

Rachel and Kylie look at each other with raised eyebrows. They know who sent them.

"He's just using you, Holls. He has no honor. You don't know the Blackstones like I do." Kylie says.

"And I don't know Holly," Rachel says. "You might be a liability for our team."

It sounds as if Rachel's voice is a million miles away as she gabbles on about my relationship with Jasper Blackstone and how my head hasn't seemed like it was in the game. She even insults me by saying that I'm not showing up as the same brilliant journalist that she knows me to be.

All I see is the color red. "Can I have those?" I ask.

I think Rachel sees in my eyes that I'm not taking no for an answer. She nods.

I collect all the offensive photos off the wooden coffee table that's shaped like a half moon. I hate how they feel in my hands. Once I have the last picture of Jasper and Julia canoodling, I turn my back on Rachel and Kylie and walk out of the office as fast as I can. I know what I have to do next.

IT HAS BEEN AGES SINCE I'VE TAKEN THE SUBWAY IN New York City, but it's the easiest way to figure out if I'm being followed or not. On the way over, I try to make sense of those photos in my head. I take them out of my purse and study each photo carefully. In this one, Jasper and Julia seem to be attending an event. They're facing each other, looking down as if they're laughing at something. The disturbing part of this photo is that they appear perfectly at ease with each other. Then I go to another photo. They're in a she-she apartment, taking a selfie while sitting on the sofa. Again, they're the picture of the perfect couple. In another photo they're in a desert, a blue and red rock mountain is their background. *They traveled together?* I'm so angry, I feel like I have enough strength to ring Jasper's strong, manly neck.

Nope... As they say, a picture tells a thousand words. I was never supposed to see the photos. Not only that but last night I told Jasper about the talk I had with Rachel and Kylie and before our meeting could get on the way this morning he had already shutdown the story. I know it was him, I just do. Kylie was right, Jasper played me. I don't think he can be trusted.

Remember that, I wait until the last minute to rush off the train at the 23rd Street stop. It's a mad dash out into the cold before the doors close. My heart beats at a mad pace as I look up and down the platform to see if I'm the only person who escaped at the last minute. I am. It's too late to see if someone is standing with their hands pressed against the window, kicking themselves for losing track of me.

WHILE I WAIT FOR THE NEXT TRAIN, I CALL A friend named Crystal Burr. She's a hedge fund manager who works in the same building as BFE's offices. I ask if she could vouch for me at reception.

"It's not one of my people you're investigating, is it?" she asks.

"No. It's personal."

I can sense curiosity in her pause. However, she chooses to vouch for me.

Crystal wants to talk and the last thing I want her to do is conveniently forget to let reception know that she's expecting me. So I hug myself nervously and listen as best as I can as she catches me up on her life. She and her husband are trying to have their first baby. She's thinking about a change in career—money isn't so sexy as it used to be. Um-hm, oh, and great are the most I say. Crystal says she read my last book, heard it was a best seller. "Lots of money." She has some great products that she'll allow me to invest in because we're friends, "Grow the surplus, not squander it."

Then, struck by illumination I put my phone back into my purse, walk across the platform, and up to the street, thinking it's best to take a cab from this point onward. If someone is tailing me, then they're probably waiting at the next stop.

"Crystal, darling, I have to go," I say as cold air blasts my face.

I thank her for the favor and yet again let her know I'll be in touch about the investment opportunity. I do have a large savings that I would like to make grow faster and larger.

I hail the first cab I see and ask him to drop me off at the building next to my final destination. Lo and behold, I swallow a gasp. I can't believe my either luck or misfortune. Jasper, wearing a suit that he didn't have on when he left my suite this morning. He looks impeccable, like he's the richest man in the world, walks out of the building. He's with a woman who's sexily wearing a knee-length trench coat. Her high heels and the black scarf coiled around her neck makes her look smart, elegant and very sexy. They stop to talk to two men, both are your run-of-the-mill businessman. Then, my jaw draws when Jasper so comfortably rests a hand on the small of Julia's back as she tosses her head back and laughs.

The hand on the back is one of the most intimate touches a man can make. It says, you're mine. It warns other men to keep away.

"Miss, this is your stop?" the cab driver says.

Eyes filled with tears, I chirp, "No. Sorry." And then ask if he could take me up to Columbus Circle. I've changed my mind.

———

MY LEGS TURN TO JELLY, AND I FALL DOWN ON THE sofa in the lobby. I need to regain some focus. Kylie was right, I don't know him at all. Actually, I don't even know where he lives. I bet Julia knows where he lives. She probably lives with him in that house or apartment where they posed like two people in love for the camera. We declared our love for each other last night, which is probably a little fast but it's what my heart feels. And I'm the one who put it in jeopardy of being broken yet again. I feel like a fool. I'm ready to cry my eyes out but not in front of the people sitting around me, who are presumably happier than I am as they wait for something or someone.

I force myself to stand, drag myself to the elevators, and walk into the next available car. Every part of my body feels heavy by despair, and my head throbs as if someone is clubbing me. How could I have been so stupid? Last night felt so authentic though. But the photos don't lie. On top of that, the way they stood next to each other in front of the building, they're obviously a real couple. It's time to go back to Philadelphia and lick my wounds. I don't know how I'll ever recover.

As soon as I step out of the elevator, my phone rings. I look at the number on the screen. It's Branson, my investigator. I let his call go to voicemail. At the moment, I don't want anything to do with a Blackstone investigation.

Each step down the hallway feels heavier than the last. *Don't cry yet.* I want to keep it together until I'm in the privacy of my own room. Once I make it to the door, I stand straight up. What if my key doesn't work? What if Rachel decided to make it official and fire me and then called the front desk and told them I'm no longer welcome in the room? My heart beats out of my chest as I slide my room key through the reader. The green light flashes as the door beeps. I sigh with relief. At least something is going my way.

I walk into the room and make sure the door is closed behind me. Suddenly, I feel something hard against my neck, squeezing. Then I feel a hard body against my backside. It's a man. It can't be Jasper. There's no way in the world he could've gotten here before I had. I try to say help as I pull at the fingers pressed against my neck while gasping for more air.

I'm being flung around and then I see a man sitting in the armchair, illuminated by the light from the floor lamp. It's Arthur Valentine.

"Let her breathe," he says in a voice that sounds like he's ordering pizza.

The brawny man releases the pressure around my neck, and I cough until air flows freely through my windpipe again.

"Do you see how fast and easy I can kill you?" Valentine asks, sitting in the arm chair with his skinny arms crossed like he owns the world.

I've already figured out that he's not here to kill me simply because he's threatening me with the possibility. So I don't scream. The worst thing I could do is piss off two aggressive men, who could easily overpower me. They have a tendency to use sex as punishment.

"But I wouldn't kill you." He stands casually. "I would kill your boyfriend. He's the thorn in my side."

"Then what are you doing here?" I ask.

"Be careful," Valentine hisses.

My heart pounds like thunder as he closes the distance between us. The man definitely isn't aging gracefully. He's pasty and has a round basketball belly. His entire face is falling. He looks like a man who doesn't care how bad he ages because, repulsive and all, he can always pay beautiful women to have sex with him.

Suddenly, he's in my face and rubbing his hand up and down my crotch. "There's the cunt young Blackstone can't keep his cock out of. Hey, Jer, how about we give it a test drive?"

The guy who's holding me grinds against me with his hard cock.

Instead of being afraid, I grew angrier. "You would be raping my corpse because you would have to kill me first," I say then clench my lips. I meant that.

Valentine smirks as his cold gaze seizes mine. He's still rubbing me, but his fingers might as well be air. Disgust makes me numb. Also, I'm thinking about how fast I can get out of this mess. If I have to fight, then I'll have to outthink these two brutes.

Finally, Valentine grunts and steps back. It's not time to sigh with relief yet. Jer's stays hard, though.

I can tell he was eager for his boss to give the order to rape me.

"Stay away from Jasper Blackstone," he finally says. "If I have to track you down again, Jer is going to fuck you silly."

So many replies race through my head, but none of them will come out. I'm just so happy to see Valentine walk to the door and open it. His disappointed hoodlum grinds against my ass one more time, and then says, "Um…" before leaving. I hadn't realized how foul the man's breath is until he lets go of me.

When the door closes, I rush over to it and lock all the bolts. My legs grow weak, and I slide against the door until my butt collapses on the floor. Now, I can do it. I cover my face with my hands and wail into my palms. But I don't know what I'm crying about anymore. I'm just sad, frightened, and definitely heartbroken.

THE CRYING WILL NOT STOP, AND I CAN'T MOVE. So many minutes, perhaps a few hours, have passed. My face is drenched. At some point I will have to grow silent, get up, and pack. I will have to make my flight first thing in the morning and abandon this wretched city.

Knock, knock, knock.

I stiffen and then stay still and quiet.

"Holls, it's me, Kylie," she says from the hallway.

I spring to my feet and race and fumble with locks until I'm able to open the door. Not until I see her face do I realize how frightened I look. I throw my arms around her, holding on to her for dear life.

"Shit, Holly, you're shaking."

"Arthur Valentine was here."

She leans back to see my face. "He was here?"

I nod rapidly. "He threatened me."

"Shit." She takes me in a hug again. "Are you okay?"

I close my eyes, but I can't stop the tears from streaming like a waterfall.

Kylie walks me to the sofa then orders us cobb salads and a tuna melt to share from room service. She swears by the food items. She says she's been at the hotel long enough to know what to order and what not to order. Meanwhile, she pours us wine from what's left over from last night's bottle.

"I'm so sorry about what Valentine and his

goon has done to you. At least now you know that nothing but bad surrounds Jasper Blackstone."

I nod stiffly, looking into her eyes. She seems so content. It's as if she's trying to hide the fact that the fissure between Jasper and me has made her ecstatic.

Kylie brings the glass of wine to her lips. "Where did you go when you left the office this morning?"

I shake my head as I gaze off, focusing on nothing. "You're right about Jasper. I loved him though." My voice cracks.

Kylie grunts dismissively. "You couldn't have loved him. You haven't known him that long. How long has it been, a month?"

I close my eyes to take the sting out of her words. For some reason they don't penetrate into me as deep as they should. I don't think Kylie will ever understand.

"The thing is…" I close my eyes as my tears fall liberally.

"The thing is what, Holly," she snaps.

Why is she so angry? I don't let her anger stop me from trying to make her understand what Jasper and I had. "The thing is it was different between us—immediate. And I've heard about instant connections. It was like he vexed me somehow."

Kylie explodes into mocking laughter. "Give me a fucking break, Holls. He played with your head. That's what he does. Count your blessings that you found out what he's really like before he really vexed you."

I snap my attention back on her. "Why do you hate him so much?"

Kylie purses her lips like a petulant child refusing to speak.

There's knocking on the door. Room service delivers our food. After collecting our salads and half a tuna melt we settle back on the sofa. It feels like our earlier conversation has been stuffed in a trunk and put away for another day. Also, the human ability to protect us from bad experiences kicks in and what happened with Valentine and his goon is starting to leave me.

"Do you have an update on Chattanooga?" Kylie asks and then bites into her tuna melt.

I rolled my eyes. "Are you still dead set on ruining the Blackstones because I'm over them?" *Maybe.*

Her eyebrows furrows then evens out. Seconds tick by. "No. I thought about it and you can't for the love of good journalism let Chattanooga fall through the cracks."

I roll my eyes, shaking my head. "Well, you're going to have to ruin the Blackstones on your own. I'm going back to my life before all of this."

"This is your life before all of this, Holly," she says, shaking her hands emphatically.

"No, it isn't. The only time I want to hear about Blackstone is on December twenty-fifth."

"Okay then, well, pass the details of Chat-tanooga on to me. I'll work that angle."

I turn my head slightly. "I thought you were forbidden to investigate the Blackstones."

"I am," she snaps. "But we're so close." Kylie seriously looks possessed by whatever keeps her obsessed about the Blackstones.

I lean toward her. "Close to what?"

She leans away from me.

I spear lettuce with my fork and hold it. "What's the real reason behind your obsession with the Blackstones?"

"I'm not obsessed."

"You are obsessed."

Our stare down is of epic proportions. However, I can see that whatever she's hiding won't be revealed this afternoon. But I care for Kylie, I truly do. Also, it's because of her that I feel so much better after being accosted by Valentine and *Jer*, whose fucking hard cock haunts me like a destructive ghost. Once again the memory of him grinding me sends a shiver down my spine and bile to my throat.

But for some reason, I feel as if I have to manage Kylie regarding Chattanooga. She could send me ten steps back if she takes another trip to the neighborhood, finds Nel, and starts asking questions. I feign a sigh of defeat. "Okay, I'll look deeper into Chattanooga."

She claps her hands once. "Yes."

"Don't celebrate yet. My lines dried up as of yesterday, but I have my investigator working on getting me a fresh catch."

Kylie nods, smiling thankfully. I can see that my investigation means something to her. I wish she would tell me why.

"Maybe one day soon, you'll let me know why you have such a vendetta against the Blackstones," I say.

Her eyes narrow to slits. "Maybe. But I don't want to think about it right now. I just want results."

Follow The Lead

HOLLY HENDERSON

Yesterday evening, Kylie was hesitant about leaving me alone, but I assured her I would be okay. I planned to lock the double bolts on the door. She told me to call her the first moment I felt afraid and she would be at my door in a matter of minutes. She also went to security to check and see if they had any images of Valentine and "Jer" entering and leaving the building.

While trying to fall asleep, Jasper called me twice. The first time I turn my back on the device and put a pillow over my head. I wasn't strong enough to hear him lie to me. The second time he called, I turned off my cell phone. I was sort of surprised he hadn't called the phone in my suite. I tossed and turned for a while before falling into a deep sleep. Even though my life is falling apart, the last two days have been draining. That's why I slept so well.

This morning, to my surprise, Bart's breakfast arrives. I think twice about sending it back but decide to keep the blue crab eggs Benedict with hash browns and winter fruit salad. Even though I feel as if I'm betraying my heart, there's no way I'm sending the breakfast away.

I force myself not to think of Jasper as I eat and return Branson's call. He says he's found my girl and then sends me the PayPal invoice to receive the information. As soon as I pay, he texts me the name Eve Bradley along with her work address, home address, and brand-new phone number.

"But I couldn't find any verifiable information on her place and date of birth," he says. "When that happens, I get a red flag."

"She's hiding something," I say, hugging my cellphone closer to my ear. I do that when I get very excited about a lead I'm hearing about.

"Bingo."

Branson and I leave it at that.

I GET DRESSED QUICKLY, DECIDING TO GET TO LONG Island, New York as soon as I can. I haven't changed my mind about going home today. I'll have to call Rachel at some point and let her know that she doesn't have to stress about firing me because I quit.

I fish my notebook out of my computer bag along with a pencil, sit at the desk in the living room, and copy the information Branson sent me word for word. I double-check what I copied, and then delete the text. I bundle up—coat, hat, scarf and I put on my comfortable ankle boots. No more corporate clothes for me, I didn't like dressing so business-like for the past two days.

I knew there were eyes on me. I'm not sure if Jasper's tail is still following me, but I'm positive Valentine has eyes on me. For him to do what he did yesterday, he is very desperate for his daughter to marry Jasper. I leave my suite, I take the stairs down as far as I could. When I encounter a locked door, I walk back up a flight of stairs, enter a new floor, and search for any sort of elevator, preferably a service one that I don't need a staff keycard to use. Finally, I find that elevator, and take it down to the basement floor. The doors slide open, and I walk out into a cement-floor hallway. I pad down the corridor until I see an exit sign above a door.

I enter a tight alley. Sweating and overheated, I relish the cold air. Soon, I'm on the move again and enter the back floor of another building. I end up exiting the lobby of a bank. The city is in full swing as I look around, trying to see if by chance anyone is watching me. I don't think so.

My cell phone rings as I plod past storefronts. It's Jasper again. This time I answer it.

"What?" I say sharply, halted by a red walk sign.

"Why haven't you answered my calls?"

"Because you're a liar Jasper."

"What?"

"You lied to me about your relationship with Julia."

The walk sign turns green and I race across the street.

"What are you talking about?"

"I saw the pictures. And I saw the two of you together yesterday in front of that building. I'm done with you. Don't call me again." I end our call.

I walk a few more blocks up the busy street. Only now do I realize that it snowed pretty good last night. Thank goodness it's not snowing now. When I reach the YMCA, I order a Lyft to take me to the grocery store where Eve works. As I wait, Jasper keeps calling. The only reason I don't turn off my device is because I need to track my ride with the app.

My cell phone dings and it's a message from Jasper.

Where are you going?

My chest turns tight and I check up and down the street. *How does he know I'm on the move?* The coast looks definitely clear. I shift from one foot to the other and hug myself to stay warm. It's so damn cold out here. Finally, a small electric vehicle stops in front of me. The window rolls down and he asks if I'm Holly Henderson.

I show him my ID, and he unlocks the back door for me. The atmosphere in the driver's car is warm and quiet. But then I remember it's not safe to just turn my phone off after getting into a stranger's car.

I have no idea what Eve looks like. Branson said it will take a few more days to get her driver's license or passport. I only know she's a cashier. I didn't even know if she's working this morning. But if she's not at the grocery store, then I'll go to her house.

The driver is not a talker, thank God. I look out

the window without really seeing anything at all. I'm exhausted by my expedition to escape the hotel without being seen. I also can't get Jasper out of my mind. It felt good to yell at him on the street corner. Although, hearing his voice set sparks of love through my heart. He sounded totally caught off guard by the accusations. He really hurt me bad. Jasper was good at infiltrating my life in order to neutralize me as a threat. At least I don't feel like a fool. He played the game of distraction and won. I'm the loser.

Traffic sucks, and nearly an hour later, we exit the expressway. Soon we are securely in the suburbs. I wonder if Eve is married and has children. Maybe she wants me to keep my distance to protect her family from her past. She and Alexia are still friends, though. Apparently, they used to get high in the woods. So she must not want to get that far away from her bad childhood or tumultuous teens.

I take a deep, steadying breath when the car pulls into the grocery store's parking lot. It's showtime.

"We're here," the driver announces.

I undo my seat belt. "Would you mind waiting?"

He sighs. "Okay. Just don't be long." He's crabby.

I smile at him. "You want anything while I'm in there?"

Thankfully, he smile slightly. "I'm fine."

I nod briskly and slide out of the back seat. Once I'm out, I scan the half-empty parking lot. A light layer of snow covers the ground. The new snow in Manhattan hasn't reached Long Island yet, but I could smell it coming in the air. I could always smell the snow. I hate the snow. My next move, which will be sooner rather than later, would be to somewhere warm, somewhere more laid back too. All of a sudden, everything I ever loved about the East Coast turns into everything I hate about it. I can thank Jasper for that.

I walk into the store, and breathe in the warm air which feels divine on my face. Soft music plays in the background. Shoppers were intensely focused on what they were doing. Heck, nobody wants to be out shopping in this weather. I'm sure each person wants to get what they came for and get home as soon as possible. I get a grocery basket just to look like a real shopper. I grab the first few items I see, and put them in my cart. My next step is to walk up to the friendliest-looking checkout clerk and ask about Eve. I plan to tell the nice person that I want to thank Eve for being such a help the other day when I came into the store then ask, "Is she here?"

The first register is manned by a woman, who doesn't look happy to be working this cold and icy morning, so I skip her line. The next register is being worked by a man. He looks nice enough, but he's doing a price check for a customer who's reading from a mailer. I can't see the face of the third checker, only the back of her head. She's blond and has shoulder-length loose curls. For some reason the hairs on my arms stand at attention. I'm eager to see her face. So I stand still, waiting with bated breath.

Finally, the woman angles her face more in my direction, and I get a good look at her profile. She must feel my eyes on her because she turns to glance at me.

I gasp as I put my hand over my mouth. It takes me a moment to let my shock subside.

"Bryn?" I call. The woman doesn't look at me again.

"Holly," a familiar voice says from behind.

I quickly turn. It's Jasper, and his attention is split between me and the cashier.

Who is Eve? The story continues in **_Claimed_**, the final book in Jasper and Holly's story.

Printed in Great Britain
by Amazon